M000307335

THE

SUICIDE

PRINCESS

By

ANTHONY BRYAN

Copyright © 2013, B.A. Wood Books

All rights reserved. No part of this book may be used or
reproduced in any manner whatsoever without written
permission, except in the case of brief quotations embodied in
critical articles or reviews

ISBN: 0615877540
ISBN-13: 978-0615877549

The Suicide Princes is a work of pure fiction. Any similarity to
actual events or resemblance to any real persons, living or dead,
is purely coincidental.

Cover photography courtesy of Taylor Reeve and
TaylorSays.com

Fan Information, visit: AnthonyBryanAuthor.com

ACKNOWLEDGMENTS

Cover photography provided by Eric McCoy. Cover shoes, "Royal Hearts," designed by Taylor Reeve and available through TaylorSays.com.

Editorial Services provided in part by Ellie Folden of Love N. Books and Stephanie Medeiros

CONTENTS

FROM THE AUTHOR

Throughout my entire life, even when I was a young child, reading has always been an escape from reality. It was a way to temporarily leave the boring monotony of day-to-day life, and it allowed me to visit far off lands, meet unusual characters, take incredible adventures, and even learn about the very edges of our universe. Being able to take my love of reading and transform it to a passion for writing has been the greatest gift I have ever received.

I hope, more than anything, that the coming pages provide an escape for you, and I hope they take you on a journey you won't soon forget. My goal is to give you something different, refreshing and new. In a sea of authors going by their first two initials and pumping out the same cookie-cutter stories, I can only try to be the one who stands out and takes you on one hell of a ride.

Find your favorite reading spot, pour yourself a drink (or two), and love every second of *The Suicide Princess...* After all, I wrote it for you!

Anthony Bryan

1
Chance Encounter

Stephanie sat in her office as Bill Webber, a robust man in his early fifties, entered through the door. The sign just outside her door read, "Stephanie Bradford, Assistant District Attorney," but the office did not seem very lawyer-like at all. In fact, the office was more of a glorified cubicle, and there were stacks of paper and jam packed manila folders surrounding the small desk in the middle. Although the room was a mess, it was more of organized chaos than anything else.

"Bradford, the Gonzales case goes to trial next Thursday. Are you going to be ready?" he asked.

Stephanie replied, "Ready to win this one, Mr. Webber."

"That's what I want to hear, Bradford. Just remember, you don't need to feel like you're in this alone. I know you're still learning the ropes, and if you need a hand, just ask."

"I will, Mr. Webber, but I think I'm ready."

"Good. Good," Webber said as he walked away.

Stephanie had finally finished law school and successfully passed the Massachusetts State Bar Exam. Working in the Suffolk County District Attorney's Office wasn't proving to be the lavish law career she had envisioned while in school, but being in the heart of downtown Boston's legal community put Stephanie right in the middle of where she wanted to be. Granted, she was only prosecuting misdemeanor crimes and minor felonies, but she knew she was on the path to being in a private law firm within a few years. At that moment, however, future plans were the last thing on Stephanie's mind. It was time for her daily lunch with her favorite co-worker Karen.

Stephanie and Karen had a lot in common, and the pair was quickly becoming close friends. The two were both new, female attorneys in their late twenties, they had many common interests, and they made each other's lives more enjoyable when dealing with the twelve-hour days that were all too common in the District Attorney's Office.

Karen was attractive, but she could be more accurately described as "cute" than anything else. At just under five feet tall, Karen was extremely petite and very slender. Her fair skin, blue eyes, and short blonde hair all combined to create an attractive appearance, but it was Karen's outgoing and bubbly personality that set her apart in any crowd.

Ready to go, Stephanie clutched her purse in her hands as she popped her head into Karen's equally unimpressive office. "Are you ready for lunch?" Stephanie asked.

Karen replied, "Holy crap, it's lunchtime already? I am completely slammed, hon. I can't go today."

Stephanie pleadingly begged, "Please come. Please. I hate walking down there by myself."

"I really can't go today, Steph. I'll never get out of here tonight," Karen explained. "But wherever you are going, will you bring me back something?"

"Okay, but I hate you! I'm going to Tony's. Want me to bring you back a number seven?"

Karen laughingly said, "Yes please, and I love you!"

"Well, I still hate you," Stephanie joked as she walked from Karen's office.

Stephanie made the ten-minute walk through Boston's Government Center to Tony's Pizzeria. It was the end of April, and although the Boston air still had a mild chill, spring had sprung, and the city was alive with activity. Trees were blooming, birds were chirping, and the air had a fresh scent that was only around during the brief Massachusetts spring.

Stephanie arrived at the pizzeria only to find an unusually long line that exited the restaurant's door. *Just great*, she thought to herself.

As Stephanie was waiting in line, she began to send a text to her husband, Jacob. She hadn't completed typing the first line, when she was interrupted by a voice, "Excuse me, but is that the new iPhone?"

Stephanie hesitantly replied, "Yes, it is," to the strange man standing behind her. Stephanie never meant to be cold to people, but being a very attractive woman placed her in the position of finding herself frequently approached by men, and being cold was the only way to deal with them. Stephanie was twenty-nine years old and quite attractive. She stood just under five foot six, weighed one hundred and twenty pounds, and had a perfectly proportioned body with natural 34C breasts. Her long chestnut brown hair, brown eyes, naturally olive tanned skin, and perfect body made her the constant focus of male attention. She was certain this question about her phone was destined to become just another pick-up attempt.

The male spoke again, "I was thinking of upgrading to that phone. Would you mind if I took a look at yours?"

Stephanie found the request innocent enough, so she obliged by handing him her phone. As she handed him the phone, he grasped it with his left hand and extended his right hand in a gesture to offer a handshake. Feeling utterly annoyed by this point, Stephanie asked, "Are you trying to look at my phone or trying to pick me up? Because..." as she waved the back side of her left hand in front of the stranger, showing him her wedding band.

"No, no, no," he said, "Nothing like that. I was just trying to be polite. My name's Derrick," he said as he extended his right hand again.

"Fine. Nice to meet you, Derrick. I'm Stephanie," she said as she reluctantly shook his hand.

Stephanie quickly noticed that Derrick was not only a quite attractive man, but she was taken aback by how well put together he was. From his trimmed goatee to his thick, combed back hair, he was meticulously groomed and dressed and obviously had a very keen sense of style. He wore a custom fitted dress shirt, slacks, brown Allen-Edmonds shoes, and stylish glasses. The sleeves on Derrick's shirt were partially rolled, and Stephanie saw his arms were tattooed to his wrists beneath a beautiful and elegant Rolex watch. Derrick had the aura of the tough, edgy, bad-boy type, but wrapped in a classy, cleaned up package, and he radiated the slightest scent of Calvin Klein cologne. Stephanie would have been lying if she said she wasn't at least slightly intrigued by the man in front of her.

The line moved slowly, and after thirty minutes, Stephanie finally reached the counter to place her order. By that time, through his apparent charm and unique sense of humor, Derrick had melted Stephanie's cold barrier, and he had her laughing and giggling.

Stephanie received the food she had ordered for Karen and her, and she was preparing to leave the pizzeria. She said to Derrick, "Well, thank you for keeping me company in line.

"The pleasure was all mine," he said with a smile.

Stephanie paused for a moment before leaving and asked, "Well?" as if she were expecting something from Derrick.

"What? Do you want my phone number?" he asked.

"No, I want my phone."

Derrick laughed and said "Oh shit, I'm so sorry. I almost forgot about it," as he reached into his pants pocket and produced Stephanie's phone. As he was handing the phone back, he said, "Well, since you didn't want my number, can I have yours?"

"Nice try, Romeo," she said as she took her phone and walked away.

Stephanie activated her phone and glanced momentarily at the unfinished text to Jacob. She looked back towards Derrick, and rather than continue her text, she deleted it. As she made the walk back to the District Attorney's Office, Stephanie thought about Derrick and how he made her feel so attractive in the way he had approached her. There was nothing sleazy or obnoxious about his come on; it was actually cute. She was amazed at how she felt about herself after such a short conversation with a complete stranger. Although she tried her very best to conceal it, the feeling Derrick gave her made her smile.

Stephanie got back to the office, and her lunch with Karen ended quickly. She returned to her own office to begin preparing for the upcoming trial when her phone vibrated, alerting her of an incoming message. The message from a telephone number she didn't recognize read, **"Hey, pizza girl! -Romeo"**

Stephanie softly spoke the words, "What the hell?" as she realized it was Derrick texting her. She responded by asking the sender if it was in fact Derrick, and he confirmed her suspicion in his next message.

She asked, **"How did you get my number?"**

"Remember when you gave me your phone? Toward the end of our conversation, I realized I was having a lot of fun with you, and I sent myself a text message from your phone."

Stephanie was far more disturbed by Derrick's action than she was charmed, and she replied, **"Asshole, I told you I am married! Please don't text me again!"**

She angrily put her phone on her desk as she said to herself, *what a jerk!*

Derrick responded by apologizing and explaining he meant no harm. Despite Stephanie's aggravation with Derrick, he was able to draw her into a texting conversation, much as he was able easily able to chat her up at the pizzeria. His charm continued to shine, and even though it was now through text messages, Stephanie eventually found herself enjoying a conversation with him once again.

The conversation went back and forth for a little over two hours, and Stephanie found herself feeling giggly again, just as she felt after leaving Derrick at lunch.

Derrick sent a text stating, **"If you want a word of advice, there is an easy way to stop irresistible men like me from hitting on you..."**

"Oh and what is that?" asked Stephanie.

"Stop looking so sexy," Derrick texted.

Stephanie replied, **"Sexy? LOL! That's a joke! My hair was a mess, I didn't even put makeup on today."**

Derrick said, **"I was referring more to your clothes. Your tight skirt, your heels, your thin top... I'm still thinking about all of them."**

Stephanie reminded Derrick, **"I'm married, bad boy. Keep it clean!"**

"What if I don't want to keep it clean?" asked Derrick. In his next message he continued, **"What if all I want to talk about is you and your naughty little office girl clothes."**

"I'm not naughty. I'm a good girl, and I'm a VERY good girl at that," replied Stephanie.

"Well, if you were in my office right now, I'd have to give you some bad girl lessons," Derrick told Stephanie.

At that moment, Stephanie knew with every ounce of sense that she needed to stop her conversation with Derrick. At the same time, however, a feeling was churning inside of her -- a feeling which she had not felt in quite some time. It was a feeling of anxiety, excitement, and curiosity. Stephanie stared at her phone for a moment and her thumb hovered back and forth between the options to reply to the text or to delete the conversation. Temptation defeated good sense, and Stephanie hit the reply key.

"Bad girl lessons, huh?" She asked.

Derrick sent back, **"We could call it something like Naughty Girl 101."**

"So what would be my first lesson?"

Stephanie waited anxiously for Derrick's response, which came quickly,

"Your first lesson would be a brief presentation," he said. **"I'd have you lay back on my desk, and I'd tell you to slide your skirt up with your legs spread wide. I'd tell you to pull your top up, exposing your beautiful breasts, and then have you start rubbing yourself through your hot little panties."**

"Mmmmm, I love this lesson so far," replied Stephanie.

Derrick's next message came, **"Then I'd tell you to pull your panties to the side, and you'd do everything I tell you to with those fingers, just like a real bad girl. Put them anywhere I tell you, and do exactly as you're told."**

Stephanie, becoming more and more excited by the thought of performing for this man she hardly even knew, was starting to become extremely aroused. She quickly penned the words "On a conference call" on a piece of paper which she taped to her office door. She closed and locked the door, and returned to her seat in which she slid back from the desk. Stephanie slouched down in the seat, and she raised her skirt as if she were actually in front of Derrick. She slid her left hand down the front of her black lace thong as she gripped her phone in her right hand, eagerly waiting for Derrick's next text to arrive.

The following message read, **"I'd want to lean back and watch you please yourself. Your shirt hanging half off, your tall black heels on my desk, your fingers working your hot, wet, pussy... I'd want to watch it all."**

"I'm doing that right now for you. My office door is closed, and I'm doing exactly what you're describing. Tell me more," Stephanie instructed Derrick.

He wrote back, **"I'd tell you to keep going until I heard you breathing rapidly, until I saw your legs starting to shake, and until I saw your face turning flush red. I'd tell you to keep going until I knew you made yourself explode."**

"Once I did, what would you have me do next?" she asked.

Derrick told her, **"I'd slide my chair back, and have you get on your knees in front of me..."**

Stephanie waited for the next text, and she could only imagine what was to come. She began to masturbate herself vigorously as she imagined what Derrick was going to describe next. She gripped the phone tightly in her right hand as the fingers on her left hand found all of her favorite spots. Her legs spread wider, and her hand worked faster as she imagined Derrick telling her to take him into her mouth, which he did in his next text. Stephanie came closer and closer to orgasm as she read each line of Derrick's vivid descriptions of the oral sex she would be performing on him. She imagined her head being guided up and down by Derrick's grip as he told her how he was dying to explode in her mouth.

He wrote, **"Look me in the eyes as I cum in your mouth, bad girl,"** and Stephanie came to the edge of orgasm.

Suddenly, there was a pounding on Stephanie's door, and Webber's voice echoed through the thin office wall, "Bradford, are you in there?"

Stephanie sprang to her feet and clumsily stumbled on her heels as she raced to pull her skirt down. She nearly knocked a set of files to the floor, and she stopped to take a deep breath. *Oh my God*, she thought to herself as she said, "I'm here Mr. Webber. Just give me one second."

Stephanie opened the door for Webber, and he could immediately see she appeared frazzled. He suspiciously asked, "Who were you on a conference call with?"

Stephanie explained, "I wasn't really on a call, sir. I was just working on this case, and I needed some time to be left alone."

Webber replied, "Look at you. You look like a mess! If you need help with this case, please let me assign someone to join you. Don't feel like you have anything to prove by jumping into the deep end of the pool so quickly."

Webber had been with the District Attorney's Office for nearly thirty years, and he never left for private practice. Stephanie knew Webber was a good man, and she knew he was very interested in helping her to become a good attorney. She told him, "I promise you, I'm ready."

Webber left Stephanie's office, and she picked up her phone. She saw that Derrick had continued to text her, and while the additional texts sent were very sexy, Webber's interruption had knocked Stephanie back into reality. She sent Derrick a text which read, **"I'm so sorry, but I can't do this. Honestly, you have no idea how much you had me turned on, but I don't even know you, and I'm married. I just can't be doing this."**

Without any argument, Derrick replied, **"I know, and I understand. If you ever want that bad girl lesson, you have my number."**

Stephanie scrolled through the text, and clicked on the option to delete the conversation. In the list of options, she also saw "Save Contact." She paused for a moment, then clicked the option, saving Derrick's number under the name "Jenna." She then deleted their conversation.

Stephanie left her office late that evening, and she walked the three and a half blocks to the parking garage where she parked every day. As she walked to the garage, and throughout her forty-five minute drive home to the suburbs, her mind was focused on Derrick. She was split evenly with one half of her feeling extremely guilty about the conversation she had with him. She imagined how she would feel if she learned Jacob had the same conversation with another woman, and the guilt grew. The other half, however, felt sexier than she had felt in years, and the feeling was driving her wild. This time good sense prevailed, and she vowed to never speak with Derrick again.

• • •

Stephanie arrived home, and as she walked through the front door, she was greeted by Jacob. Jacob, who was lying on the couch, called out to her, "Hey sweetheart, I'm in the living room watching a movie."

At five-foot-nine, Jacob stood just below average height, and he was in moderately decent shape with just the hint of a spare tire forming in his midsection. While he was in the military, Jacob took excellent care of himself and maintained a great physique, but those days have since passed, and he was settling into being comfortable with life. His light brown hair was kept short and slightly scruffy, and it suited his hazel eyes nicely.

Stephanie walked into the living room to find Jacob sitting on the couch. Leaving her black heels on, she sat on the coffee table directly in front of him. She leaned back, gently spread her legs, and said "How about you turn the television off, and I'll give you a different kind of show." In her mind she felt that it would only be fair to her husband if she allowed him to enjoy what Derrick only got to fantasize about.

Jacob replied, "I'm sorry, but I'm just not really in the mood tonight. I had three really long flights today, and tomorrow I have an overseas with an overnight. I'll be back on Thursday, and I'll take you up on that offer then?"

Stephanie closed her legs, and reached forward slipping her shoes from her feet. She said, "Your loss, but if you change your mind, I'm all yours." Stephanie knew Jacob wouldn't change his mind, so she drifted off into the bathroom for a long shower.

As the bathroom filled with steam, and the hot water poured down upon her tired body, Stephanie began to cry. For as long as she could remember, her life was constantly building towards something more. Junior high school was building up to high school, which lead to college, which lead to law school, which was for the purpose of being an attorney. Now that she was finally an attorney, she was absolutely miserable in her job and once again building up towards something else. She was exhausted and just ready to be where she wanted to be. Her marriage to Jacob was much of the same, and she felt their relationship was always a series of steps towards something different. She wanted, more than anything, to enjoy her husband in the present moment and not later in life.

After her shower, Stephanie and Jacob got into bed together and began talking about their respective days. Between Stephanie's new job and Jacob's career as an airline pilot, the two often found themselves catching each other on the go, and the end of the day was often the only time they were able to talk.

"What's wrong" Jacob asked. "I can always tell when something is on your mind."

Stephanie replied, "It's a lot of things. I'm just really tired, and I don't want to talk about it."

"Don't hold anything in, that only makes it worse. Come on, talk to me." Jacob encouraged.

"It's not just any one thing. For starters, I hate my job. I busted my ass in law school, thinking that I would come out as some hot shot lawyer, but once I got there I realized I know almost nothing about being an attorney. So instead of working in an amazing law firm, like I imagined, I'm prosecuting menial cases, from a crappy office, and I'd probably make more money if I did almost anything else. It's so frustrating."

"Remember when I first got out of the Air Force and the only flying job I could find was that shitty commuter airline?" Jacob asked. "I didn't want to work there; it was embarrassing. In the Air Force, I flew some of the largest jets on the planet, and then suddenly I'm flying a small seventy-two passenger jet between Providence and Long Island. You know you remember how much I was making there. What was it, less than fifteen dollars an hour? I stuck it out though, and I moved up. I'm not exactly where I want to be yet, but I'm getting close. And, babe, I'm happy."

Stephanie pouted, "I know, I just want to be there too. I hate this." She paused for a moment and asked, "And why didn't you want to let me be bad for you when I got home? I didn't want anything back, I just wanted to take care of you."

Jacob said in an apologetic tone, "I'm sorry. It's not you at all. I really am just so tired tonight, and I know I have another long day tomorrow. Then tomorrow night I'm in a hotel before I come home the following morning. We both knew it would be like this until I get a permanent route; we have to deal with it until then."

Stephanie knew the she wasn't just disappointed about that particular night, but all the nights, weeks, and months before. Her sex life with Jacob had eroded to virtually non-existent, but she did not feel like arguing. Instead she simply said, "You're right. I love you."

Jacob gently kissed her on the lips, his kisses were always so gentle, and he said, "We'll be there soon. We'll have all the time in the world together, we can start working on having kids, and we'll be happy."

Stephanie replied, "Yeah, we'll be happy." She waited for Jacob to fall asleep, and she finished the task she had started in her office earlier that day. She tried desperately to imagine herself with Jacob while masturbating, but it was the images of Derrick which made her tremble. The text messages were deleted from her phone, but the mental image of being Derrick's "bad girl" was burned into her memory.

• • •

The following day, Karen joined Stephanie for lunch as usual. They were eating at an outdoor cafe located on a bustling city street along Boston Common. Droves of pedestrians were passing by, and the sidewalk was damp from an earlier morning rain shower. The scent of the rain still lingered in the air, and the two women were talking when Stephanie asked Karen, "Can I tell you something?"

"Of course, you can tell me anything," said Karen. "Ooh wait, is it something good?"

"Please Karen, just promise that you won't tell anyone," Stephanie pleaded. "I need to tell someone, and you're the only person I trust with this."

Karen, becoming more serious, asked, "Is everything okay?"

Stephanie hesitatingly said, "I met a guy yesterday..."

Karen waited for a moment and asked, "You met a guy, and?" Stephanie paused longer until Karen said, "Oh you MET a guy!?!"

Stephanie was clearly embarrassed and said, "Be quiet!"

"You dirty whore!" Karen said with a kidding tone. "Details, I want details."

"Nothing happened; we were just texting. But it wasn't just texting, it got so hot. That's what is bothering me about it. It bothers me that I could get so turned on by someone who isn't Jacob."

Karen said, "Look, I don't want to know any more about it because things like this always end badly. You didn't go too far, so just stop now, and don't go any further. I mean come on, it's not like you fucked the guy; you texted him -- big deal!"

"I know, you're right," said Stephanie.

Karen quickly responded, "Now that that's out of the way, tell me about him! Was he cute?"

Stephanie then proceeded to tell Karen the story of how she met Derrick at the pizzeria. She explained, "It's not so much that he's cute, it's how he talked to me. I don't know how to describe it. He just seemed to say the perfect things at the perfect times, and I don't know, I've never talked with someone like him. Then our text messages, oh my God, he had me so incredibly turned on!"

Karen said, "It's not a big deal; he's your fantasy guy."

"My fantasy guy?" Stephanie asked.

"Yes, you're fantasy guy. I have one. Well, a few actually, but my favorite is Kevin from the Public Defender's Office. Think of it this way: how long have you and Jacob been together?"

Stephanie answered, "We've been married for just two years, but we started dating my first year of law school."

Karen replied, in a reassuring manner, "You two have been together since you were basically kids. You can only be with someone for so long before it becomes boring, and sometimes you need a fantasy guy to light your fire again. Just keep him as your *fantasy* guy, and nothing more. Don't screw your marriage up over some guy just because he can text nasty. Don't text with him anymore, and don't let it go any further, okay?"

"I won't," replied Stephanie.

"Promise me," demanded Karen.

"I promise you, I won't talk to Derrick again." Stephanie continued, "But me and Jacob haven't just become a little boring, it's almost like he has no interest in me at all. He is always 'too tired,' and he would rather play video games or watch a movie than have sex. And before you come back with 'maybe you need to spice things up,' I've tried so hard. Lingerie, watching porn with him, you name it and I've tried it."

"You've tried everything?" Karen asked.

"Everything," declared Stephanie. "It sucks, because every other aspect of our life together is amazing. When I was an undergrad before I met Jacob, I dated some very, ummm, *fun* guys. They all turned out to be assholes, but they were so fun in bed. I miss that raw naughtiness with a man."

"Have you ever tried it from behind with Jacob, but you know, the other way?" Karen asked slyly.

"Okay, maybe not everything - that's just gross," replied Stephanie.

Karen continued, while chewing her food, "Oh give me a break. Sometimes you just have to bite into the pillow and take it. It's not that bad, the first dozen times. Alright, it is that bad, but just try it."

Stephanie made a scrunched up face and said, "You're so gross, Karen."

Stephanie's conversation with Karen was suddenly interrupted by the waiter whom neither Karen nor Stephanie noticed to be standing right behind them. He said, "I really hate to kill this lovely conversation, but can I bring you ladies anything else?"

The two girls laughed so hard, and Karen nearly spit her half-chewed food onto the table. Stephanie, with her face burning red, answered, "No, we're fine, just the check would be great."

The waiter replied, "That's too bad. I was hoping you two were going to stick around for a while."

Lunch ended, the girls got back to the office, and once again Stephanie was alone with her thoughts. She knew her husband was going to be away for an overnight flight, and she would have the evening all to herself. She scrolled through the contacts in her phone until she came to the name *Jenna*. Stephanie fought the urge to text Derrick, and she put her phone down before resting her face in her hands. The confusion was more than she wanted, and she tried her best to pretend Derrick didn't exist.

• • •

Two weeks later, Stephanie hadn't had any contact with Derrick, but she thought about him every day. One evening, she was making her long drive home, and as she traveled down Massachusetts' Route 24, the traffic was thick and had slowed to a crawl. Stephanie thought about her conversation with Karen, and she let her mind wander about ways to reignite the intensity with Jacob.

She thought of the pornography she had watched with Jacob in the past while they were dating, and she tried to recall the scenes which turned her husband on the most. Stephanie's first thought was having a threesome with another woman for him. This had long been a secret fantasy which she always hoped to one day fulfill. She immediately thought of the idea of her, Jacob, and perhaps Karen when she realized that she was never going to share her husband with a woman who was such a close friend.

Stephanie then thought of begging Jacob to ejaculate on her face as she knew he was coming close. She had let men do that in the past, but Jacob had never asked to, and perhaps her begging him would turn him on. Stephanie never enjoyed having that done to her, but she also knew that she could easily pretend to love it and do it in a way that would drive him wild. Stephanie then thought to herself, *I want to be very bad for him*, and she decided to let her husband do something she had never allowed.

Stephanie arrived home, and lured Jacob to the bedroom. Jacob kissed her softly, as he always did, and the two undressed one another. Jacob pulled Stephanie's top over her head, leaving her hair in a mess as the shirt passed by. He reached around, unzipped the back of her skirt, and it loosely fell to the floor. Stephanie slipped her heels off, and the two continued their foreplay on the bed.

As expected by Stephanie, she could sense Jacob's lack of interest, and she knew he was only participating to keep from fighting with her again. Stephanie then rolled to her hands and knees and decided to surprise Jacob with something she had never done. In her doggy-style position, she looked back at Jacob, and she reached to the back of her thong. Stephanie pulled her thong to the side, revealing her wet pussy and tight anus. She said, "Turn me into your bad girl. Do anything you want tonight."

Stephanie watched as Jacob just looked at her in amazement, and she continued, "You can take me any way you want tonight. You can make me take it anywhere you want. Make me take it in my ass if you want -- I won't say no."

Jacob positioned himself behind Stephanie and gently grasped her hips. She held her breath, nervously waiting to find out whether Jacob would penetrate her as she was expecting. As his hips moved towards her, Stephanie bit into her pillow expecting the worst. The idea that she was willing to be so naughty for her husband made her excited, almost as excited as her texts with Derrick. Stephanie yearned to become Jacob's bad girl. Jacob entered Stephanie's vagina, and he began to make love to her from behind. Jacob made love to her at a steady, gentle pace, and there was no intensity. Stephanie told Jacob, "Be as rough as you want," and "Do anything you want to me," but her offers seemed to fall on deaf ears as Jacob never took advantage of her sexiest, most alluring offers. Jacob's thrusting only built in intensity as he was nearing his own climax, to which he ejaculated on Stephanie's back.

Upon finishing, Jacob flopped down on his side of the bed and said, "That was amazing. You are so sexy."

Stephanie remained in that same position for a short time, and she contemplated the feeling of complete rejection. She was willing to do anything to spice up her sex life with her husband, she even offered to humiliate herself by allowing him to do something she had once sworn to never try. Instead of feeling sexy and attractive, she was left with nothing but a shallow, empty feeling.

Stephanie wondered why Jacob didn't look at her as being someone erotic, and she realized that she wanted to be someone's bad girl, and at this point, she was willing to be anyone's bad girl. With her face in the pillow and Jacob's semen on her back, Stephanie's mind raced towards thoughts of Derrick. At that precise moment, an insatiable obsession began, and Stephanie felt as though she could no longer resist the temptation of what Derrick could offer.

As Jacob went into the bathroom to wash up, Stephanie reached for the damp towel on the floor to clean her back. Stephanie looked to be certain Jacob was in the shower, and she sent a one word text message that would alter her life forever,

"Lunch?"

Within moments, Stephanie received a response with Derrick replying, **"You know where. 12:30."**

An intoxicating rush of adrenaline swept through Stephanie's body as she anticipated the thought of seeing Derrick again. She barely knew this man, but he was beginning to coarse through her veins, and Stephanie hadn't felt so alive in such a long time.

Jacob climbed into bed and wrapped his arm around Stephanie. He let out a relaxing sigh and said, "That was amazing. I'm glad you loved it."

"And just what makes you think I loved it so much?" Stephanie asked.

Jacob smiled at her and answered, "I can see it in your face. You just look so happy right now. It's almost like you're glowing."

Stephanie's heart skipped a beat from the guilt she was feeling, because she knew the happiness was not brought about by Jacob. It was crushing her to know that someone other than her husband was making her feel this way, but even the guilt couldn't smother the excitement she was feeling for the following day's lunch date.

Jacob then reminded Stephanie, "Don't forget to wake me up before you leave for work tomorrow. I have an overnight again tomorrow, and I want to kiss you before you leave."

"I won't forget," Stephanie sighed as she pulled the

covers to her chin and a smile ran across her face. "I love you, Jacob."

• • •

The following morning, Stephanie took extra care when getting ready for work. She picked just the right outfit, styled her hair perfectly, and applied her makeup as if it were her wedding day. She stood before the mirror and saw herself wearing a black, pinstriped pencil skirt, a black low cut sweater, and her favorite patent leather pumps with bare, tanned legs. Her brown hair fell just below her shoulders, with perfectly styled waves. She thought, *Derrick's going to love this*.

Stephanie's morning was spent preparing for her upcoming trial peppered with interruptions from Webber. He would routinely pull Stephanie from whatever she was doing any time something of interest came into the office. He enjoyed teaching the new attorneys the craft of their trade, and usually Stephanie was eager to learn. She was having a hard time focusing on Webber, however, when all she could think about was her first date with her mysterious new friend. As her and Karen's usual lunch time drew near, Karen entered Stephanie's office.

"Well, well, well – don't we look nice today?" Karen said while looking at Stephanie. "What's the occasion?"

"Nothing specific. I just wanted to look cute today," replied Stephanie.

"Uh-huh, sure. Are you ready for lunch? I'm getting hungry."

Stephanie became visibly bashful and started to meaninglessly shuffle papers around her desk. She answered Karen by saying, "I can't today. I have a meeting at the courthouse at 12:30."

"A meeting?" Karen asked suspiciously. "I don't remember seeing anything on the schedule board."

"It just came up at the last minute," Stephanie said without looking at Karen.

Karen closed the office door as she began ordering, "No! No! No!" She continued, "Tell me you are not going to go see that Darryl guy."

Stephanie said, "His name's Derrick, and no, I'm not going to see him."

"Darryl, Derrick, whatever his name is, you're not going to see him. Steph, you promised me you weren't going to do this."

Stephanie tried to reassure Karen by saying, "It's only lunch. It's very innocent, I promise."

"Very innocent? This is the first time I've seen you wear makeup in over a month," Karen replied.

Stephanie pleaded with Karen, "Please, Karen, I need this, and I'm asking you to be my friend. I promise you, I'm in control, and I won't let it go too far." She paused for a moment before continuing, "But I need this right now. And more than anything else, I need you to be my friend."

Karen remained silent for a moment, and she replied, "Alright, but I'm warning you, this isn't going to end well. I'll be here for you, but I'm not getting in the middle of anything. Deal?"

Stephanie's face burst into a smile as she shouted, "Deal!"

At 12:15, Stephanie left her desk and started the walk to Tony's Pizzeria. As she walked, she realized that she wasn't even sure if that's where Derrick would be meeting her. Until that point, she just assumed that Derrick meant Tony's when he texted "You know where," but now she wasn't sure. Butterflies swirled through her stomach, and second thoughts through her head. However, with so much on Stephanie's mind, the walk went by much faster than usual, and before she knew it, she was standing at the entrance to Tony's. Stephanie knew it was now or never, and she grasped the cool aluminum handle in her soft hand, and she opened the door. She entered the restaurant to find Derrick waiting for her, and there was food for two already on the table.

The restaurant was an older building, and it was more designed for takeout orders than dining in. The restaurant had just six small booths, and Derrick was sitting in the booth furthest back from the door. He looked up to see Stephanie standing before him, and he said, "I hope you don't mind that I already ordered for us."

Stephanie asked, "How.. How did you know what I'd want?"

Derrick explained, "The day that I met you here, you ordered two number seven's. Being the genius that I obviously am, I assumed that you'd go for the number seven today also."

Stephanie, nodding her head in approval, said, "I'm very impressed. This is actually exactly what I would have ordered," as she sat down.

Derrick smiled and said, "I would have told you that my magic eight-ball told me, but with you being a slick lawyer, you'd probably call bullshit."

Stephanie's mood instantly changed. Her smile straightened, and she said, "I never told you I was a lawyer. How did you know that?"

Derrick chuckled and said, "Relax! I work for a private security firm, and we do various types of security and protection for CEOs and other wealthy people. A big part of what we do is background checks, and I did one on you."

"But, you don't know anything about me. You only knew my first name."

"I also have your cell phone number, Miss Attorney," Derrick said with a teasing tone. "I ran your number, and it traced back to your name. I didn't mean anything negative by it; I just need to be careful. I can't take a chance that someone would try to get close to me in order to get close to one of my clients. I take my work very seriously."

Stephanie smiled and said, "Try to get close to you? As I seem to recall, you hit on me, Mr. Romeo."

"I hit on you, or you hit on me. What difference does it make?" Derrick said. "We're here now, and that's all that matters."

"So, what's the name of this big, fancy security firm?"

"Work? We're seriously going to talk about work?" Derrick said as he shifted the conversation away from his job.

Stephanie found the circumstances surrounding Derrick to be very suspect, but it only added to the intrigue in which he seemed to be drenched. Despite sounding every internal alarm in Stephanie's head, more and more, Derrick was becoming her ultimate fantasy.

Stephanie leaned forward, and she rested her hand on top of Derrick's. She asked, "What would you like to talk about then?" as she gently brushed the tips of her fingers across his forearm.

Derrick responded by inviting Stephanie to discuss it further over drinks after work. Stephanie remembered that Jacob would not be coming home, and she had no reason to rush home that night. Without a moment's hesitation, she said, "I know the perfect place."

● ● ●

ANTHONY BRYAN

2
Jumping Off

Stephanie looked at her watch and suddenly realized how much time she had spent at lunch with Derrick. "Oh shit," she said. "I have a meeting in fifteen minutes back at the office. I have to go, but I can't wait for drinks."

As they both stood, Derrick leaned towards Stephanie, placing his hand on her hip and gently pulled her towards him. Derrick said, "I have a secret to tell you," as he shot a mischievous smile.

"Oh, do you now?" Stephanie asked. "Then, please, do tell."

Derrick moved towards Stephanie's ear, and as his lips reached whispering range, instead of a secret, he gently kissed the portion where her earlobe met her ear. Derrick then softly whispered, "I forgot what it was I was going to say," as he pulled away.

The simple kiss on her earlobe made Stephanie's heart flutter and begin to race. She smiled at Derrick and said, "I'll call you when I'm leaving work."

"And I'll be waiting for your call," Derrick replied as he walked towards the door.

Stephanie walked calmly from the pizzeria until she was certain she was out of Derrick's view. As she rounded the corner, she started running in place and giggling like a twelve-year-old. Stephanie's excitement was short-lived, however, when she realized she needed to hurry.

Stephanie rushed into the large conference room just as the meeting was starting, and Webber sarcastically announced, "It looks like we can start, now that Bradford has decided to join us. Thank you for gracing us with your presence."

"I'm sorry Mr. Webber. I was preparing over lunch, and I lost track of time."

Being the kindhearted man he was, Webber said, "Well we can't have you planning your first case on an empty stomach. So where are we, Bradford?"

"We're ready to go to trial, sir, and I'm very confident the Public Defender's Office will want to reach a plea agreement. We've already sent them the full case files and reports during discovery, but I also found a lot of case law during my follow-up research. I think they'll be crazy to challenge this, and this should be an easy one."

"Fantastic," replied Webber. "Have everything on my desk by three, so I can look it over before I leave tonight."

"I'm having everything copied now, sir," Stephanie said as she held up her phone to indicate to Webber she was in the process of typing an email.

Stephanie was creating the email to her assistant as the phone alerted with a soft vibration in her hands. She opened the text, and just as she had hoped, the sender was Derrick.

"I love what you're wearing today, but I have something hotter in mind," the text read.

Stephanie responded, **"I want to hear all about it after my meeting. Text you soon."**

The meeting continued on with each attorney providing status updates to Webber, and Stephanie sat quietly, pretending to be paying attention. Stephanie normally paid very close attention in the update meetings to learn as much as possible from the other attorneys, but today was different. Rather than contemplating case law and trial strategies, Stephanie's mind could not shift away from thinking of Derrick. Stephanie replied to Derrick's message,

"What exactly did you have in mind?"

"I was thinking black, lace-top thigh highs, a black garter belt, and barely nothing else," read Derrick's answer.

Stephanie blushed as she held her phone under the table to keep others from seeing she was texting, **"I don't think that would be appropriate attire for a bar. Do you?"**

"Maybe drinks shouldn't be at the bar then? Maybe my place is a more suitable environment," suggested Derrick.

"I think the bar is a much more appropriate environment," said Stephanie.

Derrick asked, "Why? Don't trust me?"

"I trust you just fine. It's me I don't trust ;)" said Stephanie.

"What exactly don't you trust about yourself?" asked Derrick.

"The fact that being around you makes me want to do the kind of things I haven't done in a very long time."

"Like what?"

"Honestly?" asked Stephanie.

"Yes, honestly."

Stephanie hesitantly replied, "Almost anything you wanted."

"Almost?"

"Yes, almost," Stephanie replied as the meeting came to an end.

Stephanie walked through the maze of hallways until she reached her assistant's desk where she confirmed the files Webber requested were being prepared.

"Barbara, please make sure the updated files for my case are on Webber's desk by three o'clock. He said he needs to look over them today," said Stephanie.

"I already took care of everything during your meeting, Stephanie," Barbara assured her. "It's already done."

"You are amazing, Barb!"

Stephanie was walking toward her office when she heard, "Hey, hoochie mama," coming from Karen's office.

Stephanie poked her head in through the door, "Who you calling a hooch, ho?"

Karen chuckled and asked, "Speaking of hoochies and hoes, how was your lunch with lover boy?"

Stephanie rushed into Karen's office and embarrassingly uttered, "Shut up! I don't want anyone else to know about that!"

"Oh, like anyone cares. Everyone here is fucking someone, so they don't care about who you're fucking," Karen said.

"But I do care," said Stephanie. "And I'm not fucking anyone."

"Not yet, anyway," Karen said with a smirk.

"So if *everyone* here is fucking someone, who are you fucking?" Stephanie asked while overly stressing the word everyone.

"My husband," Karen said, "and that's all you need to know."

"Whatever, ho. I have work to do," Stephanie claimed as she went to her own office.

Once behind her desk, in the privacy of her own office, Stephanie returned to the text message conversation with Derrick.

Derrick had since messaged, **"You have me curious, now. Partially about what you would do, but even more about what you wouldn't do."**

"The only two things I can think of, besides the obvious weird stuff, would be anal or finishing inside of me. I just can't do that."

"Finishing inside you?" Derrick asked.

"Yes, I wouldn't let someone cum inside me."

"Oh, that's different," said Derrick. "**Why not? Women usually love that."**

"Don't get me wrong, I do love it and this is going to sound so weird, but that's just something I could only do with my husband."

"Makes sense," Derrick said before asking, **"Have you ever done anything anal and didn't like it? Or are you just afraid to try?"**

"No, I've never even tried," Stephanie sheepishly admitted. She continued, **"I've had guys in the past try to get me to do it, but none of them pushed the right buttons, I guess."**

Derrick pointed out, **"You say no one has ever pushed the right buttons - does that mean you want them pushed?"**

"Possibly, depending on the situation. I think I'd be very turned on by a man who forced me to push my boundaries."

"How far would you want them pushed?" Derrick texted.

"To be honest, I'm not sure. I think I would just have to be in the situation and in the moment to decide. But if it was done right, I think I would want my limits pushed to the very edge. The only two boundaries I would not want to test are the two I said before."

Derrick replied, **"Very intriguing, but I do have a little bit of work I need to get done if I want to get out of here on time. Text me when you're leaving, and I'll see you tonight."**

"See you tonight," Stephanie responded.

Stephanie looked at the clock on her wall and realized it was only five minutes until four. Stephanie normally left work at five, but she was hoping to leave early today, so she could prepare for her evening. Stephanie picked up the phone, and was bringing the receiver to her ear, when Webber entered her office.

"I was just about to call you," said Stephanie.

"Well, better than that, I'm here." Webber said. "I have to say, Bradford, you did a kickass job on this case."

"Thanks, sir." Stephanie continued, "I know it's not the case of the century, and I probably put a lot more work into it than necessary, but I just want to show you that I know what I'm doing, and I'm ready for the next step.

As Stephanie made that statement, it came across as believable; however, nothing could have been further from the truth. She truly believed she had no idea what she was doing, and she was grasping at straws with every turn. She always loved challenges, though, ever since she was a little girl. Stephanie always set the bar very high for herself, and she always pushed hard to achieve every goal she set. In this instance, she was starting to believe she was in over her head, but she was never going to admit that.

To the contrary of Stephanie's thoughts, Webber was extremely impressed with Stephanie's performance and attitude. He saw Stephanie as a future asset to his team, and he knew she had an extremely bright future.

"Listen, Bradford, if the Public Defender accepts a deal on this, and you guys plea, that makes this one a win for you. I think all the ducks are in a row on your case, so I want you to throw out an offer. If your guy pleads guilty, I think you're ready for a felony."

Stephanie was stunned. She said, "Really? But I don't have enough cases to start prosecuting felonies."

Webber reminded her, "Last time I checked, I'm the Lead Attorney, and I decide when everyone has had enough experience to start working felonies. You're there, kid."

Stephanie then listened as Webber provided her with the details of a recent arrest of a drunk driver who had been in an accident in which the other driver was severely injured. Webber told her, "It's his third DUI, and we're looking at going after prison time on this one. I think you're ready for it. Do you?"

"I'm so ready, sir. I absolutely promise, you won't be disappointed."

"I know I won't be, but get your guilty plea first!" Webber continued, "You were about to call me when I walked in. What did you need?"

"Oh my God, I almost forgot about that," Stephanie giggled. "Do you mind if I sneak out early? I have a few errands I need to get done."

"After such a good job today, get the hell out of here. See you in the morning."

Stephanie gathered her things, and shouted "G'night, Karen," as she ran past her door.

Karen yelled, "Hey, where are you going?" but Stephanie didn't respond and just hurried to the elevators.

Stephanie walked to a lingerie boutique just two blocks from her office. She browsed through the small shop, looking for something special to wear for her date. Stephanie always loved red lingerie, but she recalled Derrick's request for black, and she decided to find something he would like. Stephanie knew she would not allow Derrick to fully enjoy the lingerie, but she wanted to wait for an opportunity to slyly let him peak at what was under her skirt. She wanted to tease Derrick, and she also knew it would make her feel sexy -- it was a feeling she had not had for a long time.

As Stephanie was searching for just the right thing, a sales associate asked, "Is there anything I can help you with?"

Stephanie said, "Not right now; I'm just looking."

"Any special occasion?" the associate asked.

"No, just looking for something to make me feel sexy tonight."

The woman glanced at Stephanie's left hand and replied, "Looks like your husband is in for a very wonderful evening. Let me know if you need anything."

"Yes, my husband," Stephanie said. "I'll let you know."

Stephanie thought about the woman's assumption, and she immediately realized what she was doing. Stephanie left the boutique and walked to the parking garage adjacent to her office. She sat in her car, cupping her face in her hands, and she said out loud, "What the hell am I doing?"

Stephanie sat for a moment, thinking of how to break her date with Derrick, when a text came in from Jacob.

"I'm at the airport, and we're just waiting for the plane to come in to swap out the flight crew. I'll probably be taking off in about two hours."

Stephanie replied, **"Two hours? That gives us a little time then..."**

"Time for what?" asked Jacob.

"Time to....you know. I was at the store looking at lingerie a little bit ago," Stephanie teased.

Jacob replied with a simple, **"That's good."**

That's Good? Really? That's Good? Stephanie thought.

Jacob followed up with, **"Me and some of the guys are going to grab a bite. Text you when we land. Love you."**

Stephanie stared at her phone for a moment, completely humiliated by the lack of interest from her husband. Stephanie replied, **"Love you, too. Be safe."**

Stephanie's feeling of humiliation grew until a moment later she blurted out, *Fuck this, I'm going,* followed by a text to Derrick which read,

"Corrigan's Pub on the corner of Newbury Street and Dartmouth at 6:30."

Derrick quickly responded, **"On the other side of Copley Square?"**

"That's the place," Stephanie wrote.

"See you soon, bad girl."

"But I'm not bad," Stephanie reminded Derrick.

"You're not bad.......yet. See you soon."

41

It was nearing 6:30 p.m. as Stephanie parked in an alley lot just behind Corrigan's Pub. She felt safe parking there now that it was light, but she knew she would be nervous walking back to her car at the end of the evening. Unfortunately, parking in this area was extremely scarce, and she had to take what she could find. Stephanie walked to the front of the pub when she received a text message from Derrick, **"Be there in five, stuck at a light. Meet me out front."**

Stephanie waited for a few minutes when she saw Derrick pulling up in a beautiful and loud, custom, chopper-style motorcycle. To this point, Stephanie had only seen Derrick during the day, when he was dressed in smart, business attire. Tonight, however, Derrick was dressed much different, and Stephanie loved it.

Derrick wore a pair of tattered jeans, and a gray deep-v T-shirt. The shirt revealed Derrick's muscular arms covered in tattoos all the way to his wrists, and his look was finished off with black boots and a wallet chain. Derrick's wrists were adorned with a beautiful watch on one and a thick platinum bracelet on the other. His look was purposely ratty, and it instantly turned Stephanie on.

She also took notice, once again, of the slight hint of his CK One cologne. She was always repulsed by the overpowering odor of a man wearing too much cologne, but she was lured in by the precise amount Derrick was wearing. It was a faint fragrance, seemingly worn as such, almost intentionally, to draw a woman closer for a better sense of his delicious aroma.

"Well, well, well, look at you, Mister Motorcycle Man."

Derrick smiled and said, "Hey, all work and no play makes Jack a dull boy. So, let's go play."

Derrick placed his hand in the small of Stephanie's back and guided her towards the door. Stephanie saw an open table, and she began to sit down. Derrick stopped her and said, "No, let's not sit here. I see something better back here."

Derrick grasped Stephanie's hand and led her to an open table near the billiards tables at the rear of the bar.

"Why back here?" Stephanie asked. "Everyone is playing pool back here."

"Exactly," said Derrick. "If they're playing pool then they're not paying attention to us."

Stephanie tried desperately to not think about Jacob, but Derrick's actions made it impossible for her not to compare. Any time she went out with Jacob he always had her choose where they would sit, Jacob always insisted on doing what Stephanie wanted, and he always looked to Stephanie to provide the details. She appreciated Jacob's desire to make her happy, but there was something about the way Derrick guided her that was driving Stephanie wild with desire for him. He was not controlling, but he was in total control.

Stephanie and Derrick made small talk getting to know one another for a short time, but Derrick's charm began shining through as he was beginning to draw others into conversation. Derrick's friendly banter with the server spilled into his joking with some of the guys playing pool, and before long it seemed as though he was a regular in a place he had never even been. Stephanie was amazed at his ability to talk and make friends with anyone.

One of Derrick's new friends invited him to play pool, but Derrick kindly declined, "Sorry, man. I have someone else I need to focus my attention on."

The stranger coaxingly said, "Yeah, I'd be scared, too."

Derrick glanced at Stephanie as she leaned in and said, "If you don't go play and kick that guy's ass, I'm leaving you here alone."

Derrick smiled his mischievous smile and looked to the stranger, "For money or fun?"

The stranger said, "One hundred?"

"One hundred it is, my man. Rack 'em up," Derrick said as he shook his new friend's hand.

Stephanie sipped her third drink as she watched Derrick easily defeat his new friend. At the end of the game, Derrick said, "Must be my lucky night! One hundred, right?"

The stranger pulled a fold of money from his pocket and began counting when Derrick continued, "No, no, no. It's cool, man. I had fun."

The stranger said, "A bet's a bet, and I always pay up."

"Tell you what," said Derrick. "Let me and my girl cut in for a game on the table, and we'll call it even. That's worth more than the hundred to me."

"It's all yours," said the stranger while giving Derrick a pat on the back.

Derrick reached his hand out toward Stephanie, and she grasped it tightly, intertwining their fingers. She pulled in close to him and said, "I'm your girl, huh?"

"Tonight you are," Derrick said as he shot Stephanie a wink.

"Your break," Derrick declared as he racked the balls.

Derrick then watched as Stephanie began to shoot. He stood behind her and said, "Here put your hands like this."

"Okay, and then what?" she asked.

Derrick pulled in close behind Stephanie as he was showing her how to correctly hold the cue. His lips were an inch from her ear, and Derrick took the opportunity to whisper "Did that get your panties wet watching me beat that guy?"

Stephanie turned back, smiled, and said, "It would have, if I was wearing any."

Derrick reacted by sliding his hand across Stephanie's stomach and gently pulling her back into him. He simultaneously pressed himself forward, and Stephanie felt Derrick's bulge pressing into her. Stephanie could easily feel how hard Derrick was as he said, "Feel that? That's what you do to me."

Stephanie looked around as she slid her hand down Derrick's stomach and over his crotch. She said, "I think it's time for me to leave, but I'm scared. Think you could walk me to my car?"

"It depends where your car is. This neighborhood can be awfully sketchy," Derrick said with a mocking tone.

Stephanie told Derrick, "It's in the very dark, very secluded parking lot in the alley out back."

Derrick replied, "Then I'm definitely not going back there. Look at what I'm wearing -- I might end up getting raped walking around like this," as he laughed.

Stephanie started walking away and said, "Up to you. But if you do want something bad to happen, come follow me."

Derrick watched as Stephanie took a few steps away without looking back. He looked at how her tight skirt formed beautifully around her ass, and he noticed how sexy her legs were in her red heels. It only took another step before Derrick was close in tow behind Stephanie.

The pair quickly reached the driver's side door of Stephanie's brand new white Volvo as she said, "This is me."

Without saying a word, Derrick turned Stephanie so her back was pressed against the car door. He wrapped his right arm around her lower back, and he slid the fingers on his left hand through her hair at the nape of her neck and pulled her head in and began kissing her.

Stephanie, again trying desperately to not think of Jacob, noticed how different this kiss was compared to the kiss of her husband. Jacob's kisses were always soft, slow, gentle, and deliberate. Derrick's kiss was filled with depth and passion. The way his lips met hers and the way Derrick caressed her tongue with his set Stephanie on fire.

As they were kissing, Derrick's hand slid down and began caressing Stephanie's ass. As he felt, Derrick said, "You lied, you are wearing panties."

Feeling the potent combination of Derrick's powerful sexuality and the cocktails from the bar, Stephanie started opening the car door and replied, "Then get in here and punish me."

Stephanie sat in the soft tan leather of the driver's seat, but she quickly moved herself over to the passenger's side to make room for Derrick. Derrick sat in and adjusted the seat all the way back, and the new car smell mixed with the leather interior to create a wonderful scent. The two continued their passionate kissing as Derrick's hands wandered all over Stephanie's toned, sexy body.

Stephanie started to slide over on to Derrick's lap, and she pulled her skirt up just enough so she could straddle her legs around him while facing him. Once on top of Derrick, she began unbuttoning her top, and she said, "Remember what you told me you wanted to watch the other day? That show you wanted?"

Derrick said he remembered it quite well.

"Well....." Stephanie said as she pulled her skirt even higher revealing the front of her red, lace thong. She continued, "Just watch."

Stephanie stared directly at Derrick as she unbuttoned her top further and pulled the front of her bra down. She revealed her perfectly shaped C-cup breasts, and she began massaging them with both hands. After a moment, only one hand remained on her breasts as she began to place two fingers in her mouth, sucking them to get them wet. Once her fingers were dripping with saliva, Stephanie slid her hand down the front of her thong, and Derrick watched as she began fingering herself under her panties.

As Stephanie massaged her clit, her other hand pulled and tugged on her nipples. Her head leaned back, and she began to moan uncontrollably. Derrick pulled the front of her panties down, allowing him full view of Stephanie's intense fingering of her perfectly shaved pussy. Stephanie continued until she was tugging on her nipples harder and harder, her chest became flush red, and she exploded into a body-convulsing orgasm.

As her orgasm ended, Stephanie regained control of her body, and she withdrew her fingers from her panties. She brought them to her lips as she whispered, "If only I had something to suck on," and she slid her fingers into her mouth only to withdraw them slowly while looking Derrick in the eye.

Stephanie crawled over to the passenger seat. With her knees on the seat and her ass in the air, she lowered her head into Derrick's lap. Derrick's hand found its way to Stephanie's skirt covered ass, and he began massaging and squeezing it as she unbuckled his pants. Stephanie reached in and pulled out Derrick's already rock-hard cock.

Stephanie's petite hand only further accentuated the girth of Derrick's thick cock as she wrapped her fingers around it. His circumcised head and long shaft ran down to his closely groomed pubic hair and shaved scrotum.

She slowly licked him from the base of his thick cock to the top and back down again, until she started sliding him, inch by inch, into her wide-open mouth. As the moment was unfolding, Stephanie felt completely electrified by how bad she was being. The feeling was becoming ever more intoxicating with each passing second.

Stephanie took Derrick into her mouth, and he pulled her skirt up so he could rub her bare ass. She began sucking Derrick, taking him as deep as she could, while she felt him pulling her thong down to her mid-thigh. The feeling of Derrick's fingers on her already swollen, wet lips made her body crave more. Stephanie wrapped her hand around Derrick's veiny cock and she began stroking him while sucking. His playing with her pussy was interrupted only by him suddenly pulling his hand up and delivering a hard slap to her firm ass. The sudden crack sent a stinging pain through Stephanie which only made her want more.

Derrick told Stephanie, "I want to control you."

Stephanie stopped sucking to ask Derrick what he meant, with Derrick replying, "Do you want to be my bad girl?"

"I so do," she answered.

"Then let me make you do whatever I want."

Stephanie said, "Control me," as her hand reached back to slide her heels off.

Derrick quickly grabbed her wrist and said, "Leave your shoes on. Always leave your shoes on."

Derrick then slid his left hand through Stephanie's hair, and he made a fist, grabbing hold of a handful of her thick, chestnut-colored hair. He pushed downward, indicating to Stephanie that she was to begin sucking again, and she immediately did exactly as Derrick wanted.

Derrick began guiding Stephanie's head, having her mouth work at just the pace, depth, and rhythm he wanted. Derrick was sliding his fingers in and out of Stephanie's pussy while still controlling her head. He suddenly stopped the movement and began pressing down. Stephanie began taking Derrick deeper and deeper into her throat, until she couldn't go any further.

Derrick said, "Take it nice and deep, bad girl."

Derrick then pulled his fingers out of Stephanie's pussy, and he began rubbing his index finger around the rim of her perfectly bare asshole. Stephanie quickly pulled her head upwards, and said, "No, not there. I told you not that."

Derrick said, "I want to push every one of your limits. I want to take you right to the edge. Let me take anything I want."

Stephanie resisted for a moment before submitting, and she said, "Make me your bad girl, Derrick. Make me do it."

Derrick began massaging her ass with more pressure. As she felt his finger was pressing with enough force to be on the verge of penetrating her, she placed her face into the seat, with Derricks cock against her face. Stephanie's face was scrunched, and she let out, "Holy fuck," and she groaned as Derrick's finger gently entered her tight ass.

After a moment, Stephanie returned to her task of making Derrick explode, and she continued sucking Derrick's cock as he fingered her incredibly tight ass. The sound of Stephanie's painful moan was muffled by Derrick's cock in her mouth, and the sound brought Derrick closer and closer to erupting. Stephanie began to feel his cock throb as he tightly gripped her hair once again. Derrick plunged his finger deep into Stephanie's ass, and he pressed downward on her head as he began cumming in her hot, wet, lip-sealed mouth.

As Derrick pumped the last of his load into Stephanie's mouth, he said, "Swallow every drop."

He heard a loud gulp emanate from Stephanie's throat as he removed his finger from within her. She began to sit up as Derrick said, "There really is a very bad girl in there, after all."

"You have no idea how bad this girl can be," she said while looking up towards him and using her index finger to swipe a small amount of semen from her lower lip.

"But you have no idea how much further I could take you."

"Touché," said Stephanie while pulling her skirt down and fixing her shirt. She flipped open the passenger side visor and opened the vanity mirror as she continued, "Holy shit, I'm a mess. Derrick, you are so fucking hot."

"How did you like having your first boundary tested?" Derrick asked while fixing his pants.

"Honestly?"

"Yes, honestly. And why do you always asked 'honestly?' Has anyone ever said 'no, just lie to me' to that question?"

Stephanie hit Derrick on the upper arm and said, "Shut up, you. Okay, so honestly, I hated it and loved it at the same time. I didn't really like what you were doing, but the fact that you were making me do it was just so intense."

"That could be just the beginning. Want me to push you even further – right to the very edge?"

Stephanie thought for a moment and said, "I don't want you to push me to the edge." After another brief pause, she continued, "I want you to push me to the edge and then right over it!" Stephanie leaned in to kiss Derrick on the neck as she softly continued, "Now get out of my car so I can go home, you dirty boy."

After saying goodnight, Derrick walked off, and Stephanie continued to get herself collected. A few minutes later, Stephanie heard the loud rumble of Derrick's motorcycle speeding off, and she began her own journey home. Stephanie's smile was beaming for the entire ride, and it just wouldn't fade.

Once home, although exhausted, Stephanie just couldn't stop thinking about Derrick. Stephanie walked to her bathroom and got the shower running. As the water heated, she slid off her heels, she unzipped her skirt letting it fall to the floor, and she removed her top. Just when the walk-in shower was beginning to fill with steam, she removed her bra and panties and got under the stream of hot water. Stephanie wasn't in the shower for more than a minute when she leaned against the cool tile wall and let her imagination of Derrick run wild. Water poured down Stephanie's glistening body as she masturbated to thoughts of what Derrick had in store for her.

• • •

The following morning, Stephanie rushed into work and bumped into Webber just outside her office. Webber, with a hearty smile on his face, announced, "The Public Defender accepted your plea agreement, Bradford! He's going to plead guilty this morning. You know what that means, right?"

Stephanie started bouncing up and down as she squealed, "The felony DUI is mine?"

"The felony DUI is yours! I'd like to see this go to trial by October, so even though there isn't a huge rush on it, don't sit on your ass with this one either."

"I won't, sir, I promise."

"Oh, and one more thing, Bradford. I don't want to see any plea agreements on this one. I want you to actually take this all the way to trial, no matter what the defense offers. You definitely have what it takes to prepare a case, and now I want to see what you can do in the courtroom."

"I've so got this," Stephanie said with a cocky tone.

Stephanie raced to her office and found the initial paperwork for her new case already waiting on her desk. She reviewed the police reports and found the defendant was Paul Hutchinson, who was arrested after a DUI crash in which he was the at-fault driver. The Massachusetts State Police investigation revealed Hutchinson to be more than twice the legal limit at the time of the crash, and Hutchinson's victim, the driver of the other vehicle was seriously injured in the incident. Stephanie read on to find that the victim was in critical condition and in a medically induced coma at Massachusetts General Hospital.

As Stephanie read on, and learned more details of the crash and the victim's injuries, she uttered to herself, *You're going to pay, you fucker.*

Stephanie sent a text to Derrick, telling him good morning. Derrick replied,

"When are you free for your first lesson?"

"My first lesson? lol" replied Stephanie.

"Your first bad girl lesson. When are you going to be free again so you can come over to my place?"

Stephanie excitedly replied, **"I'm not sure. I'll find out."**

Stephanie messaged Jacob, **"Hey honey! I just got a new case, and I may need to stay late at work a night or two next week. Do you have any overnights? I'll just do it then."**

Within a few minutes, Stephanie had her answer and she messaged Derrick, **"I'm free next Wednesday night."**

Derrick followed up, **"Meet me at the coffee shop at the corner of Beacon Street and Stuart Street at 8:00 on Wednesday night."**

"I'll be there with bells on," she replied.

Derrick said, **"I'll tell you exactly what I want you to wear, but it won't be bells ;)"**

"Smartass!" Stephanie anxiously wrote.

For the first time in her life, Stephanie felt as if she were no longer waiting for something to arrive, for something to happen. Her life was starting to give her everything she wanted, and everything was finally falling into place.

• • •

3

Living a Dream

On the Monday morning after her first date with Derrick, Stephanie arrived early for work, and she sat anxiously as she waited for Bill Webber to begin speaking.

"Listen up, everybody!" Webber belted out to the conference room full of attorneys. "We had a very tragic update to a case over the weekend, and I'm putting all hands on deck to get this thing put together."

The room grew silent as everyone waited for Webber to continue. "Stephanie Bradford, one of the newer attorneys in the office was originally assigned to prosecute this case, but some circumstances changed. I started to think she may be out of her league on this one, but after a lot of consideration, I'm trusting my gut and leaving her as the lead on this case. I do, however, expect everyone to give her a hand with whatever she needs. I'll let Bradford take it from here."

Webber looked toward Stephanie and gave her a nod as she stood and walked to the head of the large conference table. "Good morning, everyone," began Stephanie. "Last week, Paul Hutchinson was arrested for felony DUI after a car crash on the expressway. Hutchinson was determined to be the at fault driver in the crash, and the State Trooper doing the investigation observed numerous signs of impairment when speaking with Hutchinson. Field sobriety tests were conducted, which Hutchinson failed miserably, and he submitted to a breath analysis test. The result of that analysis indicates Hutchinson was more than twice the legal limit at the time of his arrest."

Stephanie paused for a moment, and although she was shuffling through her notes, it was clear she was trying to gain her composure. Stephanie continued, "The victim in the crash, 36 year old Michael Flannigan, was seriously injured and fell into a coma at Mass General. Last night, just after seven o'clock, Flannigan passed away from his injuries. The charges have been upgraded from injury-related DUI to DUI-Death Resulting, Motor Vehicle Homicide, and Negligent Manslaughter."

Karen, also in the meeting, interrupted, "Steph, what's the status of the arrested?"

"He's out on bail, but we spoke with the judge last night and his bond is being revoked. As we speak, Boston PD is picking him up to be held without bail until a new hearing."

Another attorney asked, "Any prior record on the arrested?"

"Yes, a lot," Stephanie replied. "Hutchinson is forty-nine, and he's had multiple DUIs over the past six years, a prior Domestic Battery, and a few shoplifting incidents when he was a kid. What stands out most in this case, though, is his prior drunk driving arrests."

Webber stood and addressed the room, "When I first gave this case to Bradford, I instructed her to take this all the way to trial, no plea agreements. I'm sticking with that same game plan. This guy is a piece of shit, and I think we owe it to the victim's family to make sure we get a maximum prison sentence on this. I think it's a great opportunity for us to let Bradford show us what she can do, she can prove to herself what she can do, and we can get justice for his family."

An attorney asked, "What kind of family does the victim leave behind?"

Stephanie responded, "He has, or had, a wife and two children. I haven't received their ages yet, but I'll be in touch with the spouse after his funeral is completed. I spoke with Webber this morning, and we're going to seek a minimum of fifteen to twenty years on this. Does anyone have any other questions?"

The room fell silent with no questions, and Webber ordered, "Okay, back to work all you lazy, no good lawyers. Go get me some convictions!"

Once only Webber and Stephanie remained in the conference room, Webber closed the door so they could speak privately.

"You're ready for this. You know that, right?" Webber asked.

"I am. I feel like I'm not, but I know I am."

"Just promise me one thing, Bradford. If you need help, ask for it. This isn't the time to show how incredible you are by taking everything on yourself. You drop the ball on this, and you ruin any chance of this man's family to get justice."

"I promise, sir." She continued, "I know I'm going to need help here, and I'll ask."

"I'm clearing and reassigning all your other cases. This is your only focus. Blow me away, Bradford."

Stephanie went to her own office and was instantly overwhelmed by the immense amount of paperwork she already had for her new case. Rather than waste time, she sat down and went right to work by sorting through the seemingly endless documents, reports, and affidavits.

Stephanie began a text message to Jacob, **"Guess what, sweetie?"** The message went on, **"The vic from the DUI crash died, and they are still leaving me on the case. I feel horrible that the man died, but I can't believe I'm still prosecuting it!!!"**

Jacob replied, **"What!? You're kidding me! See, I told you you'd start getting there. Total celebration time tonight!"**

"Celebration time for sure," Stephanie replied.

Stephanie went back to her task at hand, when Karen said, "Knock! Knock!" as she entered Stephanie's office, closing the door behind her.

"What's up, chica?" Stephanie asked.

"Okay, I'm just going to ask... Are you blowing Bill Webber or something? How in the hell did you get this case?"

"No, I'm not blowing Bill Webber. Now Bob from maintenance, him I can neither confirm nor deny," quipped Stephanie.

"Bob from maintenance? Gross! He's like eighty years old. But whatever. Seriously, how did you get this case?"

Stephanie explained, "I don't know, Bill just really seems to like me. Why, do you think I don't deserve it or something?"

"No, I didn't mean it like that. You so deserve it. I'm just amazed it didn't go to a more experienced attorney; this is a serious case. You work so hard around here, I can see why he likes you."

"Thanks, Karen."

Karen quickly diverted topics, "New subject. Did you see your undercover lover this weekend?"

The topic still embarrassed Stephanie immensely, and she blushed as she replied, "No, I didn't. We're meeting on Wednesday night after work."

"Drinks again?"

"Not quite. His place."

Karen leaned in as she said, "You dirty slut. I love it!"

Stephanie melted back, "Please don't say that, Karen. You know I'm not a slut. I just love the way he makes me feel. He makes me feel sexy, attractive, wanted. I barely even know this guy, but it's like he has a spell on me. I feel like I would be willing to do anything for him. I don't get it."

"How often do you two talk?"

"All day, every day. Then as much as I can when I get home at night."

"You get that feeling that he's just pumping through your veins, every second of every day?" Karen asked.

"That's exactly the feeling I get. I don't get it; I've never started to fall for someone this fast."

"Wait a minute - fall for someone? Is this just sexual, or are you starting to have feelings for him?"

Stephanie answered, "I know me, and I don't think I can be sexual with someone for long without falling for him. I am not leaving Jacob, and I'm going to try so hard to keep this just sexual, but there is just something about the way I feel when I'm with Derrick. I only want to live out my fantasies and get them out of my system, and then I can be happy with what I have at home."

"Please just be careful," Karen warned. "Something like this could get out of hand so easily. Make sure he's worth it before you cross any lines you can't go back on."

"Come on, I got a major felony case in less than a year. I think I can easily handle this," Stephanie said as her face lit up.

"Trust me," said Karen. "Sometimes, there's just no going back."

Stephanie saw it was nearing lunchtime, and she asked Karen, "Lunch together?"

Karen walked away and said, "You need to fly solo today, lovebird. I have work to do."

Stephanie pulled out her phone and messaged Derrick asking him if he was free for lunch. Ten minutes later, Stephanie was on her way to meet him at a little restaurant, Derrick said he'd been dying to try.

Stephanie followed Derrick's directions and arrived at a hole-in-the-wall Vietnamese restaurant near Quincy Market. She found Derrick inside looking over the menu.

"I know it may not look like much, but I've heard the food here is out of this world," Derrick said as he was standing from his seat.

Stephanie leaned in to hug Derrick, and he kissed her as she said, "Oh, I've missed you."

Derrick laughed, "It's only been a few days. I think someone's addicted." He jokingly continued, "So what's going on in the nerdy world of lawyers today?"

Stephanie said, "I'm a nerd and proud of it!"

Derrick got a serious look on his face and said, "Then talk nerdy to me, baby."

"You are so stupid," Stephanie joked. Her tone turned more serious, "You won't believe what happened at work."

Derrick mockingly said, "If I won't believe it, then don't bother telling me."

"Shut up, jerk. The victim from a case at work died, and they have me prosecuting it. It's a pretty major deal, and I can't believe they have me on it."

As Stephanie spoke, Derrick looked at her, intently. When she finished, Derrick said nothing, and Stephanie asked, "So, what do you think?"

"Honestly?" asked Derrick while looking overly serious.

"Yes, honestly," Stephanie said in a tone which showed she clearly realized Derrick was teasing her.

"I think," Derrick said before pausing for a moment. "This place smells kind of funny."

"Oh, someone thinks he's Mister Funny Man today. It may not be a big deal to you, but it's a big deal to me. After all, what are you, like a Private Investigator or something?"

"No, smart ass," Derrick said while laughing. "A Private Investigator goes peeping in people's windows trying to catch husbands cheating on their wives; I deal with private security. If someone is worth being hurt over what they have, it's my job to make sure nothing happens to them. And I think we both know the only windows I'm looking in are yours."

"Ooooh, I have my very own peeping Tom? So sexy."

"You do put on a pretty good, how should I say, performance."

Stephanie replied, "You haven't seen anything, yet," as she winked at Derrick. She continued, "Speaking of seeing things, what would you like to see me in on Wednesday?"

"You'll know in due time, sexy girl. But in all seriousness, back to your case at work. I tease, but I really am interested in what it's about."

Stephanie proceeded to fill Derrick in on her case as they ordered and ate their food. She was obviously so excited as she shared the details with Derrick. Derrick was an excellent listener, and although he always knew the right things to say, he also knew when to say nothing. In this instance, he did exactly that and Stephanie enjoyed having him pay such incredible attention to something that was so important to her.

The level of attention Derrick offered made Stephanie feel comfortable to ask, "Derrick, can I ask you a question?"

"Ask away, love," he replied as he twirled his fork through a pile of Vietnamese noodles.

"Just promise to answer me seriously. For two minutes, no jokes."

"No jokes," said Derrick. "I promise."

"You said your last name is Hanson, right?"

"It is. Why?"

"I got curious the other day, and I started Google-stalking you," said Stephanie with a smile, but her tone indicated quite the opposite.

"And you found something bad?"

"No, I didn't find anything bad at all."

He curiously asked, "So, what's the problem?"

"But Derrick, I didn't find anything good either. I didn't find anything at all. I checked Google, Facebook, Spokeo, Linkedin; I even checked Goodreads figuring maybe you like to read. I like to think of myself as a pretty good online sleuth, but with you, I couldn't find one thing. It's like you don't exist."

Derrick, apparently unfazed by the question, ate his noodles while replying, "We're eating lunch together, so either I do exist or you have one hell of a case of schizophrenia."

"No jokes, Derrick. You promised."

"I'm sorry, no jokes," he said while forcing back a smile. "What are you asking me?"

"Why do I know nothing about you? You know so much about me. I share everything with you, but you tell me nothing. Then when I look online, there isn't anything there either. Sometimes, I just feel like you're hiding something."

"I promise you, I'm not hiding anything. There's nothing about me online because I work very hard to keep it that way. You know what I do for a living, so I go to a lot of trouble to keep my electronic footprint non-existent. Everyone is out there putting every aspect of their life online for the world to see, but I'm the opposite. Maybe I'm becoming paranoid from my job, but I just choose to keep myself very guarded in that way."

"I understand that, but...."

Derrick interrupted, "And the reason I don't talk about my life is because there's not a lot there that I care to share or even remember. I grew up with an abusive, drunk father, and my mother ran off when I was twelve. I have a brother who's in prison, and a sister who's a junkie. I'm the only one who made it out."

"I'm so sorry," said Stephanie as she reached over the table to grab Derrick's hand.

Their fingers intertwined as Derrick replied, "It's the past, and I live for now. I walked away from that part of my life a long time ago. I put it in my rear-view, and I left. But if there's anything you ever want to know, ask me. I'd share anything with you."

ANTHONY BRYAN

Stephanie saw the slightest hint of a tear build in the corner of Derrick's eye as he explained himself. She felt horrible for placing him in the position to rehash such painful wounds, but in the same feeling, she felt a powerful connection growing with him. For just the shortest moment, his rugged, powerful, and confident exterior gave way to expose the vulnerability that sat just beneath his surface. Her heart melted as she reached to wipe the lone tear clinging to his eye.

She smiled and told him, "You just answered everything."

Just as their lunch soon ended, so did Stephanie's workday. She planned to stay late to get more work done, but Jacob had sent her a text asking her to please be home on time. He said he had a surprise for her, and Stephanie was dying to get home. After all, what girl doesn't just love coming home to a surprise?

• • •

It was already past sunset when Stephanie got home, and she walked up the dark walkway from the driveway to the front door. As Stephanie was walking, she could clearly smell the unmistakable odor of chimney smoke in the air, and she thought, *What's burning?*

Stephanie entered the front door and saw a note taped to the hardwood floor with an arrow pointing to the right, toward the dining room. Stephanie walked in the direction

68

of the arrow, where she saw another pointing to the kitchen. Once in the kitchen, a last arrow pointed to the rear family room, and Stephanie rushed to see what was next. As Stephanie was passing from the kitchen to the family room, she saw the fireplace glowing with a beautiful flame, and Jacob was waiting for her. In front of the fire, Jacob had a blanket spread across the floor, and the room was filled with the odor of Chinese food.

"I got us take-out Chinese and a bottle of Chianti to celebrate your big case," Jacob said from the floor.

"Oh my God, you did this for me, Jacob?"

"I did it for us. It's our night to celebrate everything we have together."

Stephanie's eyes began to well as she thought of the love Jacob had for her. She felt an enormous amount of guilt as she realized she was not in the mood for Chinese since she already had Asian food for lunch, but she did not dare indicate any lack of appreciation for Jacob's effort.

"Pour me a glass of wine while I get changed," Stephanie yelled while running toward the stairs to go to their bedroom.

Stephanie returned a few moments later wearing a white, silk camisole and matching panties. She sat down and the two began to eat, talk, and laugh about their days. Everything about the moment was perfect until Jacob asked, "What did you do for lunch today, grab something with Karen?"

Stephanie's heart skipped a beat, her stomach dropped, and a feeling of deep fear raced through her body the instant Jacob asked her the question. Her logical side knew Jacob was just asking out of interest in her day, but a flood of questions entered her mind: *Did Jacob know about her lunch with Derrick? Did Jacob somehow see a text message between them. Does he know something, and this is a trap?*

"Karen, yeah, Karen and I grabbed lunch at Marciano's," Stephanie clumsily said.

Jacob seemed to notice Stephanie's uneasiness with the question, but she quickly diverted the topic by leaning towards Jacob and seductively saying, "Lunch isn't really what I'm thinking about right now."

Jacob kissed her lips, and replied, "Lunch isn't really what I want to talk about either."

Stephanie looked to the imposing grandfather clock in the corner of the room and saw it was only eight thirty-two. She and Jacob had plenty of time to really enjoy the rest of the evening.

Jacob and Stephanie began kissing passionately, and they slid away from their food to an area on the floor between the blanket and the fireplace. He had Stephanie lay back as his hands gently caressed her body, and his lips softly kissed hers. He kissed her earlobe, and he then left a trail of soft, gentle kisses from Stephanie's neck to her chest. Stephanie pulled down the straps of her camisole, and she removed her breasts from beneath the soft silk of her lingerie. Jacob massaged and kissed each breast before quickly kissing his way past her bellybutton to the top edge of her silk panties.

Stephanie felt Jacob's hands begin pulling at the top of her panties as he was kissing her lower abdomen. As he began to slide them downward, she raised her hips, inviting Jacob to remove them completely. As she felt her underwear being lowered beyond her ankles, she was free to spread her legs wide for her husband. Stephanie felt Jacob kissing lower and lower on her stomach. She scratched her fingers into the carpet and let out a gasp as she prepared to feel Jacob's tongue pleasure her. It felt like forever since Jacob had gone down on her, and she was so excited about the feeling which was to come.

Jacob suddenly propped himself up, and he began rubbing the tip of his cock against her. He gently entered her, and rather than enjoying the moment, Stephanie's only thought was, *Are you fucking kidding me?*

Jacob began a rhythmic thrusting as he made love to Stephanie in front of the fire. Stephanie said, "Jacob, I'll do anything you want. You can do anything to me."

"I love that, keep talking, baby," Jacob said as he sped his thrusting.

Stephanie realized Jacob was taking her offer as mere dirty talk when she continued, "I really will. I'll be so bad for you. All you need to do is make me do whatever you want."

"You're bad. You're so bad," came from Jacob's mouth as his body slapped into Stephanie's, in a standard missionary position.

"I'm begging you, make me a bad girl. Make me do the kinkiest things."

"Keep going, keep going," Jacob said with a speed and tone that Stephanie knew Jacob was about to cum.

"Cum inside me. I want your cum," Stephanie said with a lack of enthusiasm since she knew they were moments away from being done.

Jacob pushed one final thrust, deep into Stephanie, and he grunted as she felt his cock swell inside of her. Jacob then rolled off of Stephanie and onto the floor next to her. Stephanie looked to the clock again, and she saw it was exactly seven minutes since she last looked. Stephanie was devastated by the thought of sex with her husband lasting only seven minutes. When Stephanie first saw the fire and the Chinese food when she got home, she thought she was a horrible person for what was happening with Derrick. However, as she now laid on her back, staring at the ceiling and listening to Jacob catching his breath beside her, she had a different thought. She was now thinking, *What else does Jacob expect is going to happen? This isn't my fault.*

Jacob and Stephanie cleaned the family room and got ready for bed. They joined each other on the living room couch, and Jacob said, "Let's see what's on the D.V.R."

Jacob scrolled through the recorded television shows, and Stephanie tried her best to pretend to be interested. If it wasn't for his complete inattention towards Stephanie, he would have easily seen something was growing distant within her. But while Jacob watched a television show, his wife sat just two feet away from him, fantasizing about another man.

● ● ●

The following morning, Stephanie was back at work, swimming in the deep end of the proverbial pool with her new case. She was completing subpoenas for medical records for Paul Hutchinson when she heard a man's voice at her assistant's desk, "Hello, I have a delivery for Stephanie Bradford."

"Right in there," her assistant instructed as a man with a large bouquet of two dozen beautiful, long stem roses walked through her door.

"Hi, are you Stephanie Bradford?"

"I am. Are those for me?"

"Yes ma'am," the delivery man said. "Just sign here, please."

Stephanie signed, and she was amazed that Jacob would send her flowers. As she opened the card, she was feeling completely impressed with the effort Jacob was obviously making. This feeling suddenly shifted when she read the note inside the card.

"Bad girl... Just one more night until we get to play. Tomorrow night is going to be all about seeing how well you can follow directions, and it will start with the second you walk through my door. Wear whatever you want over it, but I want you to be wearing black thigh highs, a black thong, black garter belt, a black bra, and, of course, your sexiest black heels. See you soon! -Romeo"

Stephanie completely melted into the moment. She was becoming mesmerized by Derrick, and she loved the way he always told her exactly what he wanted. From where he wanted to sit to what he wanted her to wear, Derrick always told Stephanie what he desired, and in turn, she was more than willing to oblige. Stephanie's urge to please Derrick was not lost in his request for the following night's outfit.

Stephanie text messaged Derrick, **"I got the flowers and your instructions. I would say 'thank you,' but rather than say it, I'll show it by following your instructions to the smallest detail. If there is anything else you desire, your wish is my command."**

"You're so beautiful, so sexy, and so obedient. You are going to make an excellent bad girl," Derrick replied. **"Work calls, so I will see you tomorrow night."**

The roses sat on Stephanie's desk for over an hour, until Scott, another attorney looked into her office. "Looks like someone is in the doghouse at home. I hope Jason's not in too much trouble."

"His name is Jacob, not Jason, and no he's not in trouble."

"I'm sorry. Jacob, Jason, same thing," Scott said. "Well, if he's not in trouble, you have yourself one hell of a guy, Steph."

"Yes, I do. You have no idea," Stephanie said, but she was clearly not thinking of Jacob when she spoke the words.

At the end of her workday, Stephanie brought the flowers with her knowing it would look suspicious if she wasn't able to take the flowers home. On the same note, however, Stephanie couldn't take the flowers home without telling Jacob where they came from. She carried them with her into the lingerie boutique near her office, and as she entered, Stephanie saw the same sales associate from her last visit.

"Hey, you! Welcome back," welcomed the associate.

"Hi, I'm back. And this time, I'm actually going to buy something."

The associate commented on the flowers, "Wow, lucky girl. Those are beautiful."

Stephanie paused for a moment and offered, "Would you like them? My car is parked like a mile away, and I can't carry them."

The sales associate smiled and said, "Someone sent you flowers, you can't take them home, and you're looking to buy something sexy – I'd be more than happy to get rid of them for you."

Stephanie turned bright red and said, "Please don't judge. I know it looks bad."

"If it weren't for flings, I'd be out of business. It may look bad, but sometimes it's fun to be bad. Let me help you pick out just the right thing."

Stephanie explained she knew exactly what she was looking for, and she told the associate about Derrick's instructions. The associate smiled and said, "This sounds like fun. I'm Amanda, by the way."

Stephanie introduced herself, and the two shopped like they were best friends. Stephanie walked out feeling as if she were going to be the sexiest woman alive the following night. Her walk back to her car was less of a walk and more of a strut.

Stephanie got home shortly past eight-thirty and found a note on the kitchen counter: "Hey babe, I went to bed early since I have an early start tomorrow. I'll probably be out of the house before you wake up, and don't forget I have my overnight flight. I'll see you on Thursday when you get home from work. Love you!"

Stephanie heated a frozen dinner, which she then ate alone as she browsed through a few clothing magazines which had come in the mail. After dinner, she showered, got into something comfortable, and sat on the couch to watch television. She sent a text to Derrick asking if he was around. The message went unanswered, and she decided to read her email before going to bed.

As Stephanie was still hoping for a response from Derrick, her imagination drifted into what the following night was going to be like. She was excited, but at the same time, she was very nervous. She wasn't worried about what she was expecting, it was the unexpected that made her stomach turn into complete butterflies. Stephanie wanted to be a "bad girl," but what if Derrick's meaning of that was quite different from her own. Stephanie knew she was not a prude, but at the same time, she also knew it had been a long time since her early college days. She wanted to please Derrick so badly. She knew how to be bad, but what if she fell short of what he was expecting? More than anything, though, Stephanie worried if she would be good enough. *What if I am just terrible at it*, she thought. *What if I don't live up to what he wants? What if I'm not good enough?"*

Stephanie navigated away from checking email, and she instead Googled "free hot porn."

A plethora of results came back, and Stephanie selected one that brought her to a free, tube-style video site. Stephanie had never watched porn on her own, and she was pleasantly surprised by the variety of videos the site offered. She noticed there were several categories, and she clicked on the link "hardcore."

Stephanie scrolled through the videos until she saw one titled, "Innocent Amateur Gets Fucked," and the thumbnail of the video showed an attractive female sitting on a couch. Stephanie thought, *this is perfect.*

Stephanie began watching the video, which was filmed from the man's point of view. The video was very amateurish, as it was simply a man holding a camera and the woman. It started with the man asking the woman several sex related questions and him asking her to strip. Stephanie skipped forward on the video until it reached a point where the woman was on her knees performing oral sex on the man. The camera was pointing downward, and Stephanie watched as she stroked and sucked his large cock.

Watching the video instantly turned Stephanie on, and she watched further until she decided she didn't want to just watch. She set the laptop down next to her, and her eyes remained glued to the screen as she slid her hand down the front of her tight boy shorts. Her fingers met her pussy, and she was already wet and fully aroused. She used the pad of her index and middle fingers to gently massage her clit in a circular motion. Her legs widened as she pressed firmly with her fingers. Stephanie started gently as she watched the blowjob being performed on her screen, but as the scene intensified, so did her own play.

Stephanie's fingers worked feverishly as she watched the cameraman and woman having sex in a number of positions. The man in the video asked the woman where she wanted him to cum, and she excitedly announced, "Cum on my face. Cum all over my face."

The woman pulled away and dropped to her knees, and Stephanie watched as the man started cumming on the woman's face. The woman not only seemed to be enjoying her facial, but she seemed to be craving each drop of the man's load, and the scene had Stephanie vigorously masturbating herself into a juicy orgasm. Stephanie took a long deep breath and exhaled as her body felt limp and numb. She reflected on the video she just watched and thought, *oh yeah, I can totally do this*.

● ● ●

Stephanie woke up in the morning to find Jacob had already left. This made it easier for Stephanie to pack herself a bag with her new lingerie since she wouldn't be comfortable wearing it all day in work. The heels she selected also wouldn't be the most comfortable for the office, so Jacob being gone made it much easier for Stephanie to pack a bag without the need to explain why she was bringing those things to work. Stephanie looked at the heels she selected for a moment before putting them in the bag, and she knew Derrick was going to absolutely love them.

Stephanie went to work, and her workload nearly took her mind off of Derrick. She was thankful for the volume of work her new case was giving her because if she wasn't so busy, her thoughts would be focused on Derrick all day. While her workload nearly kept her mind off Derrick, it didn't completely. Stephanie tried to text message Derrick throughout the day, but he never responded. The lack of response was unusual, and it left her worried.

When lunch finally came, she decided to work straight through. Karen called in sick for the day, and Stephanie couldn't stand to be alone with her thoughts for an hour. She was already a nervous wreck, and if she had to think quietly on her own, the anticipation would be unbearable. Working through lunch was the only way Stephanie was going to make it through her day.

Stephanie looked at her watch and saw it was ten minutes to five. She checked her phone, and she found she had still not received a response from Derrick. She began to worry if something had happened to him, and she thought of canceling her plans with him. She thought her night was ruined until she heard the rigid sound of her phone vibrating on her desk. It was a short single vibration, and she knew it was a text message.

"See you soon," Derrick said in the simple text.

"Where have you been all day? I've been worried sick!" Stephanie replied.

"Do you remember where I told you to be?"

"I do," answered Stephanie.

"Follow directions, bad girl. See you soon."

Stephanie closed the door to her office, and she activated the lock in the doorknob. Stephanie undressed, carefully laying her clothes on her desk so as to keep them from wrinkling. She retrieved her bag from beneath her desk, and she began to dress in the attire she bought for Derrick.

Once she was back in her work clothes and freshened with perfume, Stephanie put her makeup on. She applied just enough to be almost bordering on too much; she not only wanted to be bad, she also wanted to look the part in every way. She left her work heels on as she left the office, only putting her playtime heels on once she was safely in the privacy of her car. The wheels on Stephanie's car chirped loudly as she excitedly pulled out of the parking garage and made her way to Derrick.

Stephanie parked her car a few blocks from the coffee shop where she was to meet with Derrick. She was frustrated by having to walk so far in the heels, but she also felt lucky to have even found a parking spot at this time of day. Stephanie did everything she could to stay focused and not crumble from anxiety. As Stephanie walked to the coffee shop, she felt the stare of every man she walked past. Their gazes made her feel like they knew of the secret lingerie beneath her clothes, but in fact, it was just the sexuality she was exuding which they were picking up on. Her makeup, her strut, her heels, she was a woman any man would be happy to even fantasize about, but tonight she was all Derrick's.

Stephanie was quite early for her meeting, so she stopped into a nearby pub to grab a bite before meeting with Derrick. The bar-tender, while still wiping a pint glass dry, turned and welcomed her to the bar.

"Hi, can I get you a menu, or are you just here for a drink?" he asked.

"Do you have a Caesar salad?"

"No, I'm sorry," he apologetically replied. "We do have a house salad, though."

"Can I get chicken on that?"

"Yeah, we have chicken tenders. I can just cut a couple up and throw them in."

"That would be perfect," Stephanie said with a smile.

"And to drink?" he asked.

"Water with a lemon, please."

"Water with a lemon, and a house salad with some chicken thrown in," the bartender repeated.

"You know what," Stephanie paused before continuing, "Make it a Jack and Coke."

Stephanie knew she was going to be tested once she was with Derrick, and she knew there may be things that she might not be one hundred percent comfortable with, but she did not want to disappoint him. Stephanie recognized this as the opportunity to actually live out her fantasies, and she didn't want to look back with disappointment. She promised to remove the word "no" from her vocabulary for one night.

After she barely touched her salad, but easily washed down three cocktails, Stephanie realized it was time to go meet her fate. The bartender handed her the bill, and she passed him her debit card to pay. The bartender was back at the point of sale register, and he was just about to swipe her card, when Stephanie yelled, "Stop! Stop! Don't swipe it."

Stephanie was intent on only having a short affair with Derrick, and she absolutely never wanted Jacob to ever find out about her indiscretions. As an attorney, she was also something of an investigator, and she knew even the smallest slip up could lead to her being caught. Having her bar visit appear on her and Jacob's bank statement could be the first step to her secret unraveling, and Stephanie knew better than to leave such a clue.

"What's wrong?" asked the bartender.

"Don't use that card, please. I just realized that's the wrong one. Here, let me pay in cash."

"Cash works just fine for me," the bartender said as he returned her debit card.

Stephanie left the bar and walked to the coffee shop. She looked at her watch and she knew she was going to be right on time. The buzz of her cocktails had alleviated nearly all of her earlier anxiety, and the anxiety had shifted into complete anticipation. The heels of her shoes made a distinct clicking sound with each step.

Stephanie walked into the small coffee shop where she saw Derrick sitting on a plush loveseat in the back corner. Derrick had one ankle resting on the opposite knee, and both arms stretched along the top of the loveseat. He had a way about him that made it seem as though he felt like he owned the place, as if he were saying, "This is mine."

Stephanie walked slowly towards Derrick, staring at him as she seductively placed one foot in front of the other, wagging her hips with each step. She reached the loveseat and stood before him, standing with her legs slightly spread.

"I'm here," she said. "And I am dressed exactly as you instructed.....sir."

• • •

4
Becoming Bad

Derrick sat in the plush couch, surrounded by the pleasant odor of brewing coffee. The shop was filled with patrons, but he couldn't focus on anyone but the woman standing before him. Derrick saw Stephanie wearing a white, three-button blouse, a form fitting red skirt, and black stockings. As his gaze moved down past her legs, he saw her wearing a pair of black heels with a small platform and a five-inch heel. The heels had a buckled ankle strap, and in the back of his mind, even though he had no intention of telling her so, he knew Stephanie completely nailed it. Derrick could see the faint outline of Stephanie's black bra beneath her white shirt, and he didn't want to waste another minute.

"Sir?" Derrick asked without standing from his seat. "I like that. And just what will I call you?"

"You can call me anything your heart desires," Stephanie replied.

"For tonight, I just want to call you mine," Derrick said with a seductive tone.

"Then come take what's yours."

Derrick stood and reached his hand toward Stephanie's. Their fingers intertwined as they held hands, and Derrick led Stephanie to the door.

"Do you live close by?" Stephanie asked.

"I live in the building right next door. The doorman is kind of a pain in the ass, so if you ever visit, it's just easier to have me come down and meet you."

Derrick walked Stephanie to a large, red brick apartment building adjacent to the coffee shop. They approached the door, and a smartly dressed doorman welcomed Derrick back as he opened the door for the pair. Once inside, Stephanie was impressed by the building's lobby which was the complete opposite of the building's plain, nondescript fascia. The lobby was adorned with marble floors, beautiful brass fixtures, and exquisite art deco lighting.

"You live here?" Stephanie asked with disbelief.

"That's what my driver's license says," replied Derrick in his typical smart ass demeanor.

"I'm impressed. Being a private investigator must be paying well these days," Stephanie said as Derrick pressed the elevator call button.

The elevator doors retracted open as Derrick was responding, "I'm not a private investigator, you brat."

The two entered the vacant elevator, and Derrick pressed the button for the eleventh floor. As the elevator began its ascent, Derrick grabbed Stephanie and pushed her into the corner. The two fell into a passionate kiss as Derrick grabbed Stephanie's waist with both hands, pulling her in closer to him.

His left hand maintained its grip on Stephanie's waist as his right hand firmly grabbed her ass. "Like being a little brat?" he asked.

"Depends," said Stephanie. "Will it get me into trouble?"

"A lot of trouble," Derrick whispered between kissing her.

Stephanie gasped and answered, "Then I love being a brat."

As the elevator reached its destination, Derrick gripped Stephanie's hand and again led her as they went to his apartment. As they entered, Stephanie walked into a large, open floor plan apartment. The floors were gloss black marble, the walls were red brick, and the ceilings were black, industrial-style with exposed air vents and girders. The ultra-modern apartment was finished off with beautiful black leather furniture, and unique pieces of art and decor adorning the walls. Along the rear wall of the large apartment was a complete, fully chromed motorcycle.

"Oh my God, is that motorcycle real?" Stephanie asked.

"It is."

"Why do you have a motorcycle in your apartment?" she wanted to know. "I mean, don't get me wrong, it looks so cool, but that's just very different."

"I designed that bike myself, and then I had a custom builder make it exactly to my design. I meant to ride it, but it came out so perfect, I just couldn't bring myself to put it on the street. So, I keep it right there, where it will always stay beautiful."

Stephanie looked to Derrick and began unbuttoning the three buttons on her shirt while saying, "I'd love for you to take me for a ride some time."

"I plan on taking you for a ride right now," said Derrick. "I have to take a quick shower, but my bedroom is right there. Go make yourself comfortable, and I'll be in in a few minutes."

Derrick walked to the bathroom, closing the door behind him, and Stephanie went to Derrick's room. He had a large king sized bed, with a soft, thick, goose down comforter, and luxuriously soft maroon sheets. The room held the same ultra-modern style as the rest of the apartment, but had little decor. The room was simple, yet elegant, and it held true to what Stephanie was expecting.

Stephanie quickly removed her clothes so she would be ready when Derrick returned. She removed her shirt and skirt, and she laid on the bed waiting for Derrick. She awkwardly positioned herself in various poses, trying to find just the perfect position to welcome Derrick. She thought to herself, *stop over-thinking this, Stephanie. Think like a bad girl.*

A few minutes later, Derrick walked in to the room to discover the sexiest sight. Stephanie was laying in his bed wearing black, lace-top thigh highs, a black garter belt, a black thong, and a black bra. Her legs were spread wide, and she was looking directly at Derrick while gently playing with herself through her panties. Derrick looked to the floor, and he saw the heels removed from her feet and next to his bed.

"What are those doing down there?" Derrick asked.

"I didn't want to wear them on your bed and mess up your comforter."

Derrick walked towards Stephanie and said, "Let me explain something to you."

He placed his hand behind her head and guided her to a seated position. He then gently pulled on the back of her shoulder, guiding her forward while pulling upward on her hip with his other hand. Derrick guided Stephanie so that she was positioned on her hands and knees. He reached forward and pressed on the back of her head, pushing it towards the bed so Stephanie now had her shoulders and face on the bed with her ass high in the air.

Derrick continued speaking, "I told you tonight was going to be about following directions. Who told you to take your shoes off?"

"No one," said Stephanie feeling as if she'd let Derrick down.

"Tonight, when you do good, you'll be rewarded," Derrick said as he massaged her pussy through her panties, indicating pleasure as her reward.

"And if I don't follow directions?"

Derrick responded with a hard slap to Stephanie's ass.

"Ouch!" she yelped.

Derrick stared at Stephanie in the face-down-ass-up position. He could see her anus peeking around the string of her t-back thong, and he forcefully pressed his thumb against it as he said, "You'll be punished."

"No, no, no," pleaded Stephanie. "I'll be good, I'll be so good."

"Call me sir," Derrick instructed while giving Stephanie another spank.

"I'll be good, sir," Stephanie quickly replied.

"That's what I want to hear," said Derrick. He continued, "The position you're in right now, we're going to call that 'your position.' Any time I tell you to get into your position, this is where I want you."

"Good, because this is my favorite, sir," declared Stephanie.

"Now, get down and put your shoes back on."

Stephanie crawled off the bed and onto the floor. She sat, sliding her foot into her shoe and buckling the strap around her ankle, as she looked up at Derrick. He was standing in front of her, wearing only a towel which was hanging low on his waist. Derrick was in excellent physical condition, with muscular arms, a strong chest, and very defined abdominal muscles. As she finished buckling her heels, Derrick helped Stephanie to her feet. He kissed her lips and pulled her near as he asked, "Are you ready to push boundaries?"

"So fucking ready, sir," she replied, and they began kissing passionately.

Derrick and Stephanie kissed, and Derrick's passion was setting Stephanie on fire. The strength of his hands on her body encouraged her to pull the towel from his waist and wrap her petite hand around his growing cock. Stephanie began to stroke him as Derrick kissed her neck and chest. Derrick forcefully pulled both of her bra straps down, revealing her beautiful breasts. His hands cupped and massaged her breasts as Derrick began licking, sucking and gently biting her nipples. Derrick's actions only made Stephanie stroke him even harder until she felt he was rock-hard in her hand.

Stephanie slowly lowered herself to her knees, looking up at Derrick. "I don't want to do anything without being told, sir. What would you like?"

Derrick didn't say a word, but answered by placing his hand on the back of Stephanie's head and pulling her in. With her hand wrapped around the base of his shaft, her hungry mouth took the tip of his cock, and she began sliding her hand back and forth as her tongue swirled around his tip. Stephanie began taking more and more of Derrick into her mouth, and she increased the pace at which she was moving her head in and out. Stephanie thought of the porno she had recently watched, and she wanted to perform just as the woman in the video. Within minutes, what started as Stephanie teasing with her hand and mouth, erupted into an intense blowjob. Her head was bobbing in and out, and she was pumping his cock with her fist.

Derrick told Stephanie to stand, and once on her feet, he said, "Get into your position."

Without skipping a beat, Stephanie crawled onto the bed, lowered her head and shoulders, and made her ass wiggle to tease Derrick. She felt Derrick pull her thong to the side, and she felt his breath exhale against her as he began to kiss and nibble the back of her thighs. His lips moved closer and closer to her pussy until she finally felt his warm tongue press against her wet lips. Derrick wasted no time, and he began to lick Stephanie's pussy exactly as she loved it to be done. His tongue alternated between flat pressed strokes against her clit and a swirling motion that drove her insane.

Stephanie moaned and squealed as she panted, "Is this a reward, sir?"

"It is," mumbled Derrick without stopping his devouring of Stephanie's pussy.

Derrick pulled away and said, "Roll over and come here."

Stephanie rolled into a seated position, and Derrick moved his face towards her own. Their lips met, and Derrick delivered a deep kiss to Stephanie. "Mmmmm, so yummy," said Stephanie.

"Want to taste more?" Derrick asked.

"Yes, please."

Derrick pushed on Stephanie's chest, laying her on her back. He placed his hands on the backs of her knees and he spread her legs open. The instant his mouth met with her pussy again, she let out a moan of sheer pleasure. Derrick used his fingers to pull her lips open, and his tongue pressed into her clit once again.

Derrick continued licking and sucking on Stephanie until her breathing became deep and rapid, and her chest started to become flush red, both signs of her impending orgasm. She whimpered, "Derrick, I want to cum. May I please cum, sir?"

Derrick's response was to press harder and move his tongue faster, an indication that he wanted her to orgasm. Stephanie's body began to shake, and her foot began to convulse as the feeling built up in her lower abdomen. A feeling of wave after wave of intense orgasm rippled through Stephanie's body, and her back arched as she screamed out, "Holy fuck, I'm cumming!"

Stephanie's body settled, and she struggled for breath as Derrick stood upright. Stephanie was laying on her back, with her ass right at the edge of the bed. Derrick stood before her and asked, "What do I get now?"

Stephanie, between breaths, said, "Any damn thing you want."

Stephanie closed her eyes and relaxed into the mattress as she felt Derrick's cock sliding into her. He entered her as deep as she could take him, and he immediately began increasing the intensity, until he was fucking her so hard that Stephanie had to hold her breasts to keep them from bouncing.

"Move your hands, and let your tits bounce," Derrick instructed.

Stephanie did as she was told, and Derrick began to fuck her even harder. Stephanie, wanting to try talking dirty, said, "Fuck me, Derrick. Fuck me."

Derrick slapped the inside of Stephanie's thigh and said, "You can do better than that, bad girl."

"Fuck my pussy, baby. Fuck my hot little pussy."

Derrick delivered another, and much harder, slap to Stephanie's thigh, "Do better or it's punishment time."

Wanting desperately to please Derrick, and also very intimidated by the thought of what Derrick might do for a punishment, Stephanie belted out, "Fuck my dirty little cunt, sir. Fuck it like I'm your slut."

A smile brewed across Derrick's face as he said, "Good fucking girl. Now get back in your position."

Stephanie rolled to her face-down-ass-up position, and Derrick grabbed her hips as he entered her from behind.

She reached up between her legs and played with Derrick's balls as his cock fucked her dripping wet pussy.

"Be as rough as you want, baby," Stephanie told him.

Derrick accepted the invitation and reached towards Stephanie's head. He grabbed a handful of hair and pulled so hard he pulled her up onto her hands. Derrick continued to pound Stephanie as she was now on her hands and knees with her head being pulled back by her hair. Derrick slapped Stephanie's ass, and the slap sent a jolt of pain through her. "Slap me again, sir," was her only reply which Derrick was more than happy to oblige, repeatedly, until Stephanie's right ass cheek was stinging and glowing bright red.

Derrick pulled out of Stephanie, and rolled her onto her back. He got off the bed, placed his hands under her arms, and he dragged her to the edge. "Relax your head," Derrick said as Stephanie's head was now hanging over the edge of the bed.

Derrick stood in front of her face, and he inserted his cock into her mouth. Stephanie attempted to move her head upward to begin sucking, but Derrick instructed her, "Just let your head hang. Let me fuck your mouth."

Stephanie's fingers went towards her pussy, so she could masturbate herself while Derrick's cock plunged deeper and deeper into her mouth. After a few minutes of this, Derrick grabbed Stephanie by the hair and pulled her from the bed and onto her knees. She knelt down, looking up at him as he asked, "Who wants to get her face fucked?"

"I do," Stephanie replied.

"You do, what?" Derrick asked condescendingly.

"I want to get my face fucked, sir," Stephanie said with a hint of embarrassment.

The embarrassment in Stephanie's tone, however, was something of a facade. While she was somewhat embarrassed to actually speak the words, she was actually loving every second of her encounter with Derrick. He was manhandling her exactly as she had hoped, and she knew she was going to finger herself to another orgasm when Derrick roughly took hold of her hair and slid his cock into her mouth.

"Can you still taste your pussy on my cock?" Derrick asked.

"Mmmmm hmmmm," mumbled Stephanie as her fingers found their way to her dripping wet lips.

"Does it taste good?"

" Mmmmm hmmmm," Stephanie answered again, and her fingers began their familiar circular movement which was certain to make her cum.

Derrick, seeing that Stephanie was fingering herself, became even more turned on and began thrusting his cock in and out of Stephanie's mouth and throat at an increasing rhythm. Stephanie's face-fucking grew so intense she almost reached her limit, but at the same time, she didn't want Derrick to stop. The internal contradiction of simultaneously loving and hating something brought Stephanie to a whole other level.

Derrick suddenly pulled his cock from Stephanie's mouth, and he tightened his grip of her hair. Stephanie, coming close to orgasm herself, looked to Derrick and begged, "Please cum on my face. I'm begging you, cum on my fucking face."

Stephanie closed her eyes, opened her mouth, and let her tongue partially hang out. "Cum all over my dirty face, baby," she said as she felt the first wave of orgasm release from her lower abdomen.

Stephanie's body surrendered to full explosion as she felt Derrick controlling her head and heard his hand pumping his wet cock. She heard him grunt as the first stream of cum landed directly in her face, and her mouth opened wide as she hoped to catch the next. The second burst shot across her chin and cheek. It wasn't until the third burst that she received a mouthful of Derrick's salty load. Stephanie closed her mouth and swallowed as Derrick finished cumming on her face. With his cum running down her face and dripping from her eyelashes, Stephanie took Derrick back into her mouth to swallow the last remaining drops.

Stephanie dropped from her knees to a seated position and her back was resting against the bed. She took a series of deep breaths as she just let her body revel in that magical moment felt only after an incredible orgasm. Stephanie heard Derrick walking away, and she heard him starting the shower on the other side of the apartment. She thought, *are you serious? Did he seriously just walk away?*

A moment later, Stephanie heard Derrick walk back into the bedroom, and she felt him gently running a towel across her face. Stephanie placed her hand over Derrick's, and the two of them wiped her face together.

"That was fucking incredible," Derrick said as he helped Stephanie to her feet. Stephanie said nothing, until Derrick asked, "Are you okay?"

"I'm better than okay," she finally answered. "I'm just speechless right now. That was… That was… That was just beyond words."

Derrick laughed and said, "Let's get you out of those heels. I have the shower started for you. Go clean up, and come back in when you're done."

Stephanie walked into the bathroom and found a neatly folded towel draped across the sink for her, and the water was already hot. She detached the garter straps from her stockings and rolled them to her feet as she slid out of them. She removed the rest of the lingerie and stepped into the shower where the hot beads of water danced off her sweaty body. Stephanie was still euphoric from the last orgasm, and the steaming hot water only elevated the feeling. Stephanie felt like she could have stayed in the shower forever, never letting this feeling fade, but she also wanted to get back to Derrick.

Stephanie turned the water off, reached for the towel Derrick left her, and dried her body. She walked across the open living area towards Derrick's room, and she could see the room was lit with candles before she even entered.

"What's this?" Stephanie asked.

The room was lit by four flickering candles on Derrick's nightstand. Derrick had also straightened the bed while Stephanie was in the shower. Derrick, now wearing just a pair of black boxer-briefs, turned to Stephanie and said, "Come here, I have a surprise for you."

Stephanie, wrapped in her towel, pranced quickly towards Derrick. "What's my surprise?" she queried.

Derrick, who was holding a bottle of liquor, poured a little more than an ounce of scotch into a glass filled with ice cubes. He picked up a white pill from the nightstand and washed it down with the liquor.

"Ahhhhh, that's good," he said.

"What was that?" Stephanie asked.

"The best scotch money can buy. Well, the best scotch my money can buy; I'm pretty sure there's a lot better out there."

"Not the drink, Derrick. The pill?"

"Do you want one?" Derrick asked as he picked up another pill from the nightstand.

"No. No, I definitely don't want one."

"Derrick began pouring another glass of scotch and said, "Here, just try."

"I'm not taking anything that I don't know what it is, or where the hell it came from." Stephanie declared defiantly.

"Relax, it's a Vicodin. It will go perfect with your next surprise."

"Derrick, tonight was amazing, but I have to go home. I have work tomorrow."

Derrick said, "I think you should be sick tomorrow. That way, you can have a drink, relax, let me give you your surprise, and we can sleep nice and late tomorrow."

"I can't miss work tomorrow. I have a lot going on."

"Then just stay the night, and go to work from here."

Derrick held the drink in one hand and the pill in the other, and he extended both hands to Stephanie. She took the glass in her left hand while taking the pill with her right. She hadn't done drugs of any kind since college, and she looked at the intoxicants for a moment until she sheepishly asked, "This won't hurt me? You promise?"

"Do you trust me?" Derrick asked.

"I do."

Derrick placed his fingers on the bottom of the glass within Stephanie's hand, and he gently pushed the glass upwards. Stephanie placed the pill in her mouth and swallowed it down with the harsh liquor.

"Holy shit, that's strong," Stephanie said through a scrunched up face.

"Now for your surprise," Derrick said as he had Stephanie remove her towel and lay flat on her stomach along the edge of the bed.

Stephanie, although just having had sex with Derrick, was very shy to be fully nude in front of him. Derrick stood beside her, and he told Stephanie to close her eyes. Stephanie then felt several drops of oil fall to her back, and she felt Derrick's hands begin to massage her. It did not take long before Stephanie started to feel the intoxicating effect of the alcohol mixed with the pill, and she felt like she was floating while Derrick's hands and fingers massaged her from head to toe.

Derrick leaned in and whispered into her ear, "See? Whenever you do exactly as your told, you'll be rewarded."

"Mmmmm, I never want this to end," Stephanie groaned.

Shortly after, Stephanie fell fast asleep, and Derrick crawled into bed next to her.

"Stephanie, are you awake?" Derrick asked once he was in bed. "Are you awake?" he asked again.

Stephanie didn't respond, and when Derrick was certain Stephanie was asleep, he reached for his phone and sent a text message:

"I got her....she's done. Thank you!"

A moment later, a message returned, **"You are the very definition of a piece of shit."**

Derrick typed back, **"I'll take that as a compliment coming from you....."**

Derrick snickered as the response to him read, **"You have no idea how much I hate you."**

• • •

5
Where you Belong

The following morning, Stephanie woke from a dead sleep and sprang into a seated position. Based on the brightness of the sunlight streaming through the window, she knew she had long overslept.

"Oh my God, Derrick, what time is it?" she asked.

In a groggy, half-interested tone, Derrick replied, "I don't know. My watch is on the nightstand."

Stephanie grabbed her phone to check the time, and she not only noticed it was 11:30, she also saw she had six missed calls from Bill Webber. Stephanie tapped a few keys on her phone, and it began to ring.

Webber answered with, "Where the hell are you?"

"I'm so sorry, sir," Stephanie replied. "I am so sick today, Mr. Webber, and I can't make it in."

"And you happened not to notice how sick you were until almost noon?" Webber angrily asked.

"I tried to sleep it off so I would be better, but I took medicine around four this morning, and I guess it completely knocked me out. I'm so sorry."

"This better not happen again, Bradford!"

"I'll be in tomorrow, sir. No matter how I'm feeling, I'll be there," Stephanie said before ending the call.

"Who was that asshole?" Derrick asked.

Stephanie got out of bed and began dressing in the clothes she had taken off the night before. As she dressed she answered, "That was my boss, and he's not an asshole."

"Then why was he acting like one?"

"Gee, I don't know. Maybe because I didn't show up for work today," she replied with a sense of aggravation. "Speaking of which, don't you have a job to go to?"

"I make my own hours. I'll be there when I get there."

"Must be nice, but I actually have to answer to people."

"What the hell did I do?" Derrick asked. "You're a big girl, and you decided to not set an alarm to call your boss this morning. Don't take it out on me."

"I don't mean to take it out on you. I just – I don't know. This seemed like a good idea last night, but this morning, I'm not sure," Stephanie said as she finished packing her overnight bag. "I have to go."

"Why are you leaving? You're already here, and you already missed work, so what's the difference? We can just spend the day together."

Stephanie walked over to Derrick as he was still in bed, with the bed sheet barely covering his body. She kissed him on the cheek and said, "I have to go, Romeo. Stay in bed, I'll let myself out."

Stephanie walked to her car, and as she got closer to it, she saw the bright orange envelope under her windshield wiper. *Just great!* she mumbled to herself as she pulled the parking ticket off the window and stuffed it into her overnight bag. Stephanie sat in her car and held her phone in her hands for a few moments, just staring at an open message with Derrick. She thought about what to type, and she began the message.

"Last night was absolutely amazing," Stephanie began. **"But I don't think I can do this again. You are almost perfect in every way, but I'm married, and I can't do this anymore. I'm so sorry I'm doing this by text, but if I did it in person, I just wouldn't have the strength to say goodbye."**

Derrick responded, **"Goodbye? Is that what you're saying?"**

"Yes, Derrick. Goodbye."

"If that's what you want, I'll respect it. I think you know me well enough by now to know that I'm not the guy that's going to beg and plead. So, if you want to go, I'll step aside, but make sure it's what you

really want. If someone hurts me once, I'm not going to invite them back to do it again"

Stephanie deleted the message, and she then scrolled through her contacts until she reached *Jenna*, the name under which she had stored Derrick's number. Without the slightest pause, she deleted the contact along with Derrick's number, and she drove away without so much as looking back in her rear-view mirror.

Stephanie arrived home, and she raced to check the online flight status for the flight Jacob was flying. She saw she had at least another two hours before Jacob was home, and she began emptying the lingerie from her overnight bag. As she was pulling out the garments, she saw Derrick's brown leather belt at the bottom of the bag. She had no idea how the belt found its way into the bag, and she only assumed she accidentally threw the belt in her bag as she was picking up her own clothes from the floor. Stephanie emptied all of the contents from the bag, with the exception of the belt and the parking ticket, and she ran out to her driveway to throw them in the trunk of her car. Stephanie had no way of explaining the items to Jacob, and like her debit card at the bar, a man's belt could be the one thing to get her caught.

Breathe. Just breathe, Stephanie said to herself as she returned to her kitchen.

Stephanie hand-washed the lingerie and then placed it in the dryer on a gentle dry cycle. Once the load was dry, she put the lingerie in her drawer, she put her ultra-sexy heels away in her closet, and she breathed a sigh of relief that everything was over and cleaned up. Before long, Jacob was home.

"Steph? Are you home?" Jacob called out as he walked through the front door.

"You're home!" Stephanie squealed, running to hug Jacob.

"What are you doing home so early? It's not even five yet."

"I'm home to surprise you. I missed you and wanted to be waiting when you walked through the door." The lie burned at Stephanie's soul, but she didn't know what else to say. She continued, "Guess what!"

"What?"

"The D.V.R. Is filled with shows, I got popcorn when I went food shopping last week, and the best part of all, we have nowhere to be tonight," said Stephanie.

"Let me unpack, take a quick shower, and I'll meet you on the couch."

"I'll get the blanket and popcorn ready," Stephanie replied.

As they sat on the couch together, Stephanie curled into Jacob, and he held her tight. She knew with Jacob was where she belonged, but she struggled to keep her mind from drifting back to Derrick. Stephanie knew Jacob was who she was supposed to be with, and although her body and heart ached for Derrick, her mind knew Jacob was the right person for her.

Stephanie did her very best to forget Derrick, and she told herself she would simply chalk up her night with him as a fun life experience. However, some things are much easier said than done.

• • •

Nearly two weeks after leaving Derrick, Stephanie thumbed through the endless pile of documents related to the Hutchinson case. As she did so, she suddenly realized she had looked over more than a dozen pages without paying an ounce of attention to a single one. She was still trying so hard to forget Derrick, but she checked her phone, over and over again throughout the day, hoping he would text, but he hadn't.

Stephanie's assistant stuck her head in the office and told her, "You have a delivery!"

"For me?" asked Stephanie.

"Yes, and I think you're going to be very, very happy. I'll bring it in."

Stephanie felt like she was on a roller coaster as her stomach dropped. She knew Jacob wouldn't surprise her with a delivery at work, so it only left one possibility. Stephanie rose from her seat to run to the door to see what her assistant was bringing in.

"Here you go!" her assistant exclaimed.

Stephanie saw a large box of three ring binders and asked, "What are these?"

"I ordered you three-ring binders so you can start organizing all your paperwork. I know the office always runs low on them, so I went ahead and ordered some for you."

"Oh, thank you," Stephanie said, but her tone and expression were anything but appreciative.

"Did I do something wrong?"

"No, no you didn't. It's just me. I was half expecting...it doesn't matter, I guess. I was expecting something from someone else. I really do appreciate you getting these. I'm sorry I reacted the way I did."

Stephanie's assistant left the office, and Stephanie felt horrible about the way she reacted. She also felt horrible about the fact that she couldn't erase Derrick from her mind. Stephanie knew she needed a change of scenery, even if for just a few days.

"I have an idea," she texted Jacob.

"What's up?" he asked.

"Do you have any free flights built up from work?"

"For me, I can fly any time there's space available, but for you, yeah I have free flights saved."

"Let's go away this weekend. I'll take Friday off, so we can leave Thursday night and come back Sunday."

"I have a flight on Sunday night, so we'd have to be back by afternoon. Where are you thinking?"

"Vegas," Stephanie wrote. "I've always wanted to go."

Jacob, raining on Stephanie's parade as she had expected, said, "Vegas? We don't have the money for Vegas. Let's go to Cape Cod or something."

Stephanie, gaining a new sense of confidence in herself, replied, "I'm going to Vegas this weekend. The only question is, are you coming, too?"

After a few moments without a response, she pleaded, "Come on, this will be fun, and I think we both need this."

After Jacob agreed, Stephanie moved on to her next challenge: asking Bill Webber for the day off.

"Mr. Webber," Stephanie said as she knocked on his door jam. "I know this probably isn't the best time to ask, but is there any way I can have Friday off?"

Webber replied, "You know, every inch of me wants to tell you no, but before I do, why do you need it off?"

Stephanie sighed and explained, "Honestly, I was going to lie to you. I was going to make something up about an illness in the family, or something, but I can't do that."

"Well that's awfully nice of you," Webber said while looking somewhat surprised. "Continue."

"It may or may not be any of anyone's business, but my marriage is in a lot of trouble. I'm having some very serious personal issues at home, and I want to take a long weekend with my husband to try to fix them," Stephanie said to her boss.

"Bradford, I don't know what is going on with you lately, and I'm not sure I want to know, but you are a good attorney. You have a bright future here. If you think a long weekend will help you work on whatever you have going on in your life, then enjoy your long weekend."

Stephanie thanked Webber and sprinted back to her office to text Jacob, **"We're going to Vegas! And remember, what happens in Vegas, stays in Vegas ;)"**

● ● ●

As Jacob and Stephanie walked through the airport in Las Vegas, Stephanie felt like she was on her way to her first day of school. "Jacob! Jacob! We're actually in Las Vegas!"

Stephanie was amazed that the airport actually had slot machines in the terminal, and she stopped at the first set of machines she saw. She dug into the bottom of her purse to retrieve a small handful of quarters, and she started dropping them into machines.

"You know you're just wasting your money on those, right?" Jacob asked.

"Who cares? It's fun. Loosen up a little, and have fun. We're in Vegas, honey!"

They went on to collect their luggage and they were in their taxi when the driver asked, "Do you want me to take the strip or the side streets?"

"What's the difference?" Stephanie asked.

"The strip is going to be packed, and it will take us about forty-five minutes to get to the hotel, whereas the side street will take about fifteen. But if you two have never been to Vegas, the ride down the strip is beautiful," the cabbie explained.

"Oh definitely take the strip!" Stephanie yelled.

Jacob quickly interrupted, "No, we'll just take the side streets. I've been here a lot, and it's not really that fantastic." He turned to Stephanie and continued, "We'll get to the hotel faster this way."

Stephanie struggled to catch random glimpses of the brilliant Las Vegas strip just a few blocks over. The buildings blocking the view occasionally parted, giving her a brief view of the spectacle she was missing. The lights, the signs, and the activity, she wanted to see it all for herself. She thought, *Derrick would have taken me on the strip.*

By Saturday night, Jacob and Stephanie were in their hotel room getting ready for their last night together in Vegas. Stephanie had been in the bathroom for nearly an hour when Jacob knocked on the door, "Can I come in soon? I need to start getting ready, too."

Stephanie answered through the closed door, "I'm almost done. I promise, it's worth the wait."

Stephanie had gone into the bathroom with a bag, promising to have a surprise for Jacob when she came out. The door opened, and Stephanie came strutting out to Jacob. She wore a loose black dress that flowed just above her knees. The low-cut design showed just enough cleavage to tease while still leaving something to the imagination. She lifted her skirt slightly, raising the bottom to a mid-thigh level and just high enough to show Jacob she was wearing the same black thigh highs and garter she wore for Derrick. Jacob then noticed she was wearing a pair of black platform, spike heels; however, he had no idea she had recently worn the same heels during her encounter with Derrick.

"You look amazing," Jacob said while struggling for words. "What do you want to do tonight dressed like that?

Stephanie said in her flirtatious voice, "Well, last night we just went to dinner and a show. Tonight, let's go do something fun. I have the perfect idea."

Stephanie and Jacob took a cab to the Palms Hotel, and they walked straight to the entrance for the chic nightclub Ghost Bar. As they got closer, they saw an enormous line of other party-goers waiting to get in. Jacob asked an employee how long the wait was, and they were told approximately three hours.

"Holy shit, Steph. I'm not waiting three hours in line."

"Neither am I, wait here," Stephanie said before walking away.

Jacob watched as Stephanie went to a nearby ATM machine and dug into her tiny clutch purse. She conducted a transaction at the machine then returned to Jacob, grabbing his hand. "Come on, follow me," she said.

Stephanie walked up to one of the club's doormen, an extremely large man with a clipboard and a microphone earpiece in his ear, and she took hold of his hand. As she released his hand, Jacob saw him quickly slide something from her hand, and he slid what Stephanie passed him into his pocket. Stephanie waved Jacob over and said, "He's letting us cut the line, honey."

The doorman undid a velvet rope, allowing the couple to pass. Stephanie and Jacob heard those in the front of the line complaining as they passed towards the elevator. "Have a great evening," said the doorman as the elevator doors closed.

The elevator climbed to the nightclub located on the 55th floor. As they climbed higher and higher, Jacob asked, "What the hell did you say to that guy?"

"I just asked if we could cut the line," Stephanie said with a smile.

"And why did he let us?"

Just as the elevator reached its floor and the doors opened, Stephanie said, "because I gave him a hundred dollars."

Stephanie walked out of the elevator before Jacob could reply, and the two walked into the club. It was an impressive lounge-style atmosphere with pulsating blue/green lighting, a large bar to the right, several VIP tables behind a roped off area, and a large balcony jetting from the side of the building. The amazing views of the city from fifty-five stories were rivaled only by the views provided by the array of beautiful people in the club.

Jacob found an open table, and the two sat down. Stephanie didn't waste any time and started ordering cocktails to make her night as fun as possible. Jacob wasn't much of a drinker, and he only ordered one drink which he nursed all night. Stephanie, on the other hand, was feeling her inhibitions melt away as she finished her third drink in less than an hour.

"I want to dance," Stephanie said into Jacob's ear.

"You know I hate dancing, Steph."

Stephanie leaned back towards Jacob's ear and replied, "I know you do. I didn't say I want to dance with you; I want to dance *for* you."

Stephanie stood in her tall heels, and she positioned herself in front of Jacob. She began dancing seductively for Jacob, but he seemed more embarrassed by Stephanie than enticed. She leaned in to his ear again and said, "Relax. We don't know anyone here, and we'll never see any of these people again. Just watch me and enjoy."

Stephanie continued dancing, running her fingers through her hair, and occasionally pulling on her dress to reveal the lace tops of her stockings. Each time her dress would rise, Jacob would quickly reach to pull it down. Stephanie then stepped back, slightly out of his reach, and pulled her dress slightly higher with one hand while wagging her finger with the other, as if to say, "No, no, no."

Stephanie stepped back in toward Jacob and extended her hand towards him. He reached his hand out to Stephanie thinking she wanted to hold it. Instead, she placed his hand on the inside of her thigh, just below her skirt, and she gently pulled on his wrist to guide his hand up. Jacob pulled his hand away, and said, "Okay, I think someone's had enough to drink."

What the fuck is wrong with this guy? Stephanie screamed in her head, but the only words to pass her lips were, "Forget it, I just want to go."

A quiet cab ride was followed by a completely uneventful night in their hotel room. Stephanie laid awake in bed, and she heard Jacob begin breathing much deeper, indicating he had fallen asleep. Stephanie deeply wondered what had happened to their marriage. They had no fun together anymore, and they seemed to be growing apart from one another at a frightening pace. Most upsetting to Stephanie was that the weekend passed and her husband didn't have sex with her one single time. *What is happening to us?* she wondered. *What am I doing wrong?*

● ● ●

Back at work on Monday, Karen saw Stephanie walking out for lunch. Karen called out, "Hey, Stephanie! Wait for me!"

Stephanie stopped walking just long enough to tell Karen she wanted to be alone, and she was going for a walk.

"Are you alright?" Karen asked.

"I'm fine, hun. I just really want to be alone right now."

"Can I please come? I'm really worried about you," said Karen.

Stephanie answered, "I promise, we can talk soon. We can grab a drink after work one night, but for right now, I'm just not in the mood to talk."

Karen watched from the sidelines as Stephanie did a complete one-eighty from when she was seeing Derrick. Stephanie stopped wearing makeup again, she put minimal effort into her appearance, and worst of all, her work was slipping. Stephanie, who was once meticulous to detail in every aspect of her life, was now letting everything go. She was falling to pieces.

● ● ●

ANTHONY BRYAN

6

A Price to be Paid

Three weeks after Stephanie last saw Derrick, Karen finally cornered her into having lunch together. They were talking over their usual meal at the pizzeria when Karen asked, "How have things been with you and Jacob since you stopped seeing lover boy?"

"Things have been the same," Stephanie said with a hint of sadness. "But I guess that's a good thing. I don't know."

"Do you miss him?" Karen asked. "Do you miss Derrick?"

"So much," Stephanie said without a moment's hesitation. "I think about Derrick almost every minute of every day. I feel like I'm dying without him."

"So why did you stop talking to him?"

"I had to, Karen. I was so afraid I was going to fall for him, and I did. If it was just sex, that would have been one thing, but Derrick was starting to become the person I wanted to go to every day. I was starting to love him. I do love him."

"And that's a bad thing why?" Karen asked as she chewed her chicken sandwich.

"Because I'm married; that's why."

"I'm just saying, I don't understand why you walked away when you liked this guy so much."

Stephanie, looking perplexed, asked "Aren't you the same one who told me to stay away from him, to be careful, don't let it go too far, blah, blah, blah? It was going too far, way too far, and I had to stop it."

"Stephanie, I'm your friend. I'd never judge you or question you, and I'll always look out for you. In the beginning, yes, I thought this was a very bad idea. But something happened – when you were seeing Derrick, you were happy. You wore makeup, you did your hair pretty, you actually smiled. I saw a whole new you. Now that you've walked away from that, you're different."

"How am I different?" Stephanie asked, half expecting the answer to come.

"You're miserable, sweetie. I hate saying that, but it's true. You have been just absolutely miserable lately."

"I know," said Stephanie while choking back tears. "I miss Derrick, and the more I miss Derrick, the less I want to be with Jacob. Every time I look at Jacob, I just think that if I wasn't with him, I'd be with Derrick. I feel like my husband is stopping me from being with the one I want to love. Do you know how shitty that feels?"

Karen listened silently until Stephanie began to cry hysterically while forcing "I don't know what to do" through her tears.

"Holy shit, I can't believe I'm about to say this," Karen said while taking a deep breath. "Maybe you need to see where this is going to go with this guy."

"What?" Stephanie asked with disbelief.

"If this guy makes you so happy, this happy, maybe he's the right one for you. Maybe you've just been with Jacob for so long, you feel comfortable with him, but he's really not the one. The rest of your life is probably going to be a very long time, Stephanie, and it might be Derrick that's going to make you the happiest and not Jacob."

"I just don't know," Stephanie said while continuing to cry.

"You just completely wrote him off, and all I'm saying is that maybe that wasn't the best idea. Just think about it. Maybe you need to see where it's going to go with Derrick, or at least where it could go, before you decide anything." Realizing Stephanie was emotionally overwhelmed by the conversation, Karen quickly said, "But enough about that; we need to go back to work in a few minutes, and you can't go in looking like this."

Karen took Stephanie to the ladies room to help Stephanie fix herself. The two went back to work, and Stephanie tried her best to concentrate on her case. She had a motion-to-suppress-evidence hearing the following day, but the hearing was the last thing on Stephanie's mind. She used the Internet on her work computer to log into her mobile phone account. After a few clicks and scrolling through a few pages of her monthly statement, Stephanie saw Derrick's number.

Stephanie messaged Derrick, **"I'm 99% sure I completely blew it, but I miss you."** A moment later she followed with, **"Your bad girl misses you."**

Derrick messaged back, **"I miss you, too, but you walked away from me. I don't know if I can forgive that. I want to, but I don't know if I can."**

"I won't walk away again. I don't know how I can make all of this work, but I'll figure something out. I promise I will."

After a few minutes without a response, Stephanie messaged again, **"I'll do anything to prove how sorry I am. Anything."**

"Anything?" Derrick asked. **"I'm going to have to punish you for me to even consider forgiving you."**

"Anything," Stephanie typed. She continued, **"Any time, any place, and anything. I know I deserve to be punished."**

"And you know what I'll want."

"There are a few things that I think you'll want, and you can have all of them," Stephanie offered. "No matter what my punishment is, I'll take it."

"I want you to tell me the one thing you know I'm going to want," Derrick instructed.

Stephanie took a deep breath, and she replied, "You're going to want anal."

"And what about it?" Derrick asked.

"You can have it -- no limits," replied Stephanie.

"Tonight," Derrick instructed.

"Derrick, I can't tonight. I have to work late to prepare for a hearing, and Jacob isn't away. He's home."

"Forget it then," Derrick coldly replied. "You had your chance."

"No, no, no, Derrick. I said any time, so yes, even tonight."

Derrick instructed Stephanie to meet him at the coffee shop at six o'clock. Stephanie stared at her day planner which showed she had a five o'clock meeting in the conference room with Bill Webber and the other attorneys assisting her on the Paul Hutchinson case. Her glance shifted between her planner and the message with Derrick before she responded, "I'll be there."

Stephanie left work just before five o'clock without anyone noticing, and she turned off her cell phone to avoid the calls which were destined to begin once it was obvious she wasn't coming to her meeting. By six o'clock, she was walking with Derrick through the lobby of his apartment building.

As Stephanie and Derrick walked from the elevator to his apartment, Stephanie noticed Derrick was quite different than before. He was not his usual joking, flirty self, and he was barely even talking to her. There was no hand-holding, no welcoming kiss, and the tension was building with each passing second. Stephanie and Derrick walked into his apartment, and Derrick went directly to the kitchen area.

"Come here," Derrick said as he pulled a glass from the overhead cabinet.

Derrick opened a drawer and removed a brown prescription bottle from which he dropped two pills to the counter. He used the bottom of the glass to crush the pills into a fine powder against the cool granite counter top. Derrick brought the rim of the glass to the edge of the counter, wiped the now-powered pills into the glass, and he began to pour scotch into the glass. Once an ounce of alcohol was in the glass, he handed the glass to Stephanie.

"Here, you're going to want to drink this," Derrick said with a matter-of-fact tone.

Stephanie held the glass, just watching the powder dissolve into the concoction. "I don't want to drink this."

"Drink it or not, I don't care. But trust me, you're going to wish you had."

Stephanie desperately looked at Derrick and said, "You don't need to punish me, Derrick. I know it was stupid walking away, and I'm never doing it again."

Derrick, becoming visibly angry, said, "No, I do need to. I think you know by now, I'm not the kind of guy that gets walked on and then invites the person back for more. With me, you walk away once and you're done. I'm going against my own rule, and the only way I can feel okay about it is with this. So, if you want me to be able to forgive you and move past it, then yes, I need to punish you."

Stephanie, wanting so badly not to upset or disappoint Derrick, sheepishly said, "You're right. I deserve this," as she brought the glass to her lips.

"Why did you crush them?" Stephanie asked as she drank the last drop.

"They'll get into your system faster, and you'll feel it much better."

Stephanie placed the glass on the counter and apologetically said, "I'm sorry I'm not wearing something better for tonight, but I wasn't expecting this."

Derrick said, "It's okay, I don't want you wearing anything at all for this. In fact, take your clothes off now."

"Right here?" Stephanie asked.

"Right here."

Derrick watched as Stephanie began to undress in his kitchen. She unzipped her skirt which then fell effortlessly to the floor. She pulled her top over her head, and she stood in her underwear, nylons, bra, and heels.

"Leave my shoes on?" she asked.

"Not tonight."

The sensation and feeling of the situation was not in the least bit sensual for Stephanie, and stripping for Derrick like this felt more degrading than erotic. "Can I finish undressing in the bedroom?" she asked. "Please?"

"No, finish right here."

Without giving a verbal response, Stephanie unclasped her bra and slid it down her arms, revealing her breasts. The cold temperature of the room had her nipples firmly erect. She slipped her feet from her heels, and she bent forward as she slid her nylons and panties down her legs and to the floor in a single motion.

Derrick began walking to the bedroom and said, "Follow me."

Stephanie began following Derrick, walking behind him, when he looked back and said, "Don't walk. Crawl."

"On my hands and knees?" She shyly asked.

Derrick grabbed Stephanie by the hair, and he pulled her toward the ground. She didn't resist in the slightest, and she immediately went to her hands and knees. Derrick's right hand pulled back and belted forward with an explosive slap on Stephanie's ass. The crack echoed through the open apartment as Stephanie yelped in pain.

"And bring your nylons with you," said Derrick. We're going to need those at some point."

Derrick then walked to the bedroom as Stephanie crawled behind him. Once in the bedroom, Stephanie remained on her hands and knees and said, "I'm sorry I didn't crawl the first time you told me to. I don't want to be punished again, I'll do whatever you say."

"Is that how you think this is going to work tonight?" Derrick asked. "This isn't like last time. Tonight, you're being punished no matter what. There's no getting around that."

Derrick grabbed Stephanie by the hair and pulled her to a standing position. He turned her toward the bed and bent her forward so her bare feet were on the cold floor, the front of her legs were against the side of the bed, and her stomach was flat on the mattress. Once again, Derrick's hand reared back and delivered another slap on Stephanie's ass. Derrick repeated this several times as his hand alternated between slapping her left and right ass cheeks. Stephanie's bottom began to glow bright red as she cried out, "Derrick, I'm sorry. I'm so sorry. Please, baby, I'm sorry."

"Stand up and turn around," Derrick ordered, with Stephanie instantly obeying. "Go down on your knees."

Stephanie dropped to her knees, and began to prepare herself for what was certain to come. She remembered the last time she was in this position with Derrick and how rough he was. This time, however, Derrick was upset, and

Stephanie was uneasy about what she knew he was about to do.

Within moments, Stephanie had Derrick's hard cock in her mouth, and she was stroking and sucking to the very best she could. Her tongue swirled as she rode her lips up and down his hard, throbbing dick. Stephanie imagined that if she could make it feel incredible for Derrick, he would not take over, but her plan soon withered.

Derrick ran his fingers through Stephanie's hair, until the palm of his hand was against the back of her head. He instructed her to remove her hand, and he began to enter deeper and deeper into her mouth, pulling her head in as he went. Stephanie struggled not to gag as the tip of his cock entered her throat, and Derrick began to pump his cock in and out.

Stephanie reached her hands up to push on Derrick's thighs. Derrick quickly barked, "Put your hands behind your back," and Stephanie grabbed one wrist with her opposite hand behind her back, doing exactly as she was told.

Derrick fucked Stephanie's throat until he quickly pulled his cock from her mouth. He pulled her head in, guiding her lips towards his balls, and Stephanie knew exactly what Derrick wanted. Her tongue licked and caressed every square millimeter of Derrick's balls as her hand reached up and stroked his cock. Derrick switched, back and forth, between deep-throating Stephanie and having her lick his balls.

Stephanie gasped for breath each time he pulled his cock from her mouth, and her eyes began to water. Derrick eventually grabbed his cock and began wiping it across Stephanie's lips and slapping her face with it, an act that made her want to suck him even more.

Derrick suddenly pulled away and said, "Don't move."

Stephanie watched Derrick pick up her nylons from the floor, and she asked, "Do you want me to wear those for you, baby?"

"No, I have a better idea. Lay on the bed," Derrick said while ripping her nylons in two even halves.

Once Stephanie was on the bed, Derrick rolled her onto her stomach. He grabbed hold of her left wrist and began using the black, silk nylon to tie it to the slatted headboard. He then repeated with her right wrist.

Derrick pulled on the makeshift restraints to check their hold, and when he was satisfied, he asked Stephanie, "Are you ready to be my little slave?"

"I am," she said with a shaken voice. "I'm yours."

Derrick rolled a pillow and slid it under Stephanie's hips, with the pillow now propping her ass up for him. His fingers slid down her back, over her supple ass, and between her legs. When Derrick's fingers touched Stephanie, she felt as though someone had given him a road map to pleasing her; he knew exactly what she wanted. He began to slowly, but firmly massage and rub Stephanie's pussy, causing her to moan and squirm. Until that moment, Stephanie was so preoccupied with the fear and intimidation of her punishment, she had no idea how much it was actually turning her on.

Stephanie's mind flashed back to Derrick making her crawl across the floor, Derrick spanking her, and thoughts of his cock in her mouth. The degradation and humiliation, coupled with her hands being bound in complete submission brought her closer and closer. Derrick watched carefully as he saw her beginning to show signs of orgasm as he intensified his masturbating of Stephanie. As he saw she was moments away, he suddenly stopped.

"Please, baby. Please let me cum," Stephanie groaned.

Derrick responded, "You don't get to cum," as his left hand grabbed her hair and pulled while his right hand delivered yet another hard slap.

Stephanie's ass, already tender from her earlier spanking, began to fade as the crushed pills and alcohol were beginning to dull her senses. She felt her body begin to feel a floating sensation as the yearning for orgasm swirled through her. "Please, Derrick, please let me cum."

Derrick's fingers went back between her legs and picked up where they left off, and he began repeating the cycle of bringing Stephanie to the edge of orgasm only to stop as she was getting so close.

After several rounds of bringing Stephanie to the brink of orgasm, over and over, Derrick left Stephanie unsatisfied and begging for pleasure. She begged, "No, don't stop. I want more."

"You want more?" he asked. You're about to get a lot more."

He reached for a small plastic bottle on his nightstand, and he then repositioned himself behind Stephanie. He grabbed her hips, pulling her up onto her knees. She felt him place his left hand on her ass and gently pull as she felt drops of oil landing on her. The fear in Stephanie's body rose to a level which her earlier drink couldn't mask.

"Derrick, baby, I'm so sorry. I learned my lesson. I'm so sorry," Stephanie pleaded as she felt the tip of Derrick's cock pressing against her tight ass, and she struggled against her restraints.

"Who's my bad little whore?" Derrick demanded to know as he pressed against her with more pressure.

"I am, baby. I'm your bad little whore," Stephanie moaned, so eager to please Derrick, as she felt the pressure increase until his cock began to disappear inside her.

Stephanie bit into Derrick's bed sheet, and her hands pulled against her restraints. Derrick pressed until he had pushed as much of his cock into Stephanie's ass as he thought she could handle. He began slowly sliding out and then back in, gradually increasing the pace, intensity, and depth in which he was thrusting himself into Stephanie. This continued to build until he was behind Stephanie, holding her hips with both hands, and fucking her ass to the absolute edge of her limits.

Stephanie felt Derrick's hand reaching under her to massage her clit. Derrick's fingers in her pussy, mixed with his cock in her ass, brought Stephanie to a level of ecstasy she never imagined. She pleaded with Derrick to let her orgasm, to which he replied, "Explode for me, bad girl. I want you to explode."

Derrick continued to punish Stephanie's ass as he rubbed her pussy until it brought her to a heart racing, body sweating, muscle twitching orgasm. It took every ounce of her strength to keep her legs from giving out from under her and her body collapsing to the mattress. Stephanie, wanting desperately for Derrick to finish, screamed, "Go, baby. Fuck my ass until you cum. I want your fucking cum."

Derrick grabbed Stephanie's hair and pulled so hard her head lurched back. He grunted as he began to go faster and harder until he pushed in for one last thrust. Stephanie felt his cock swell inside her as Derrick began pumping his load inside her raw, fucked ass.

Derrick collapsed forward, resting on Stephanie. The two were panting and dripping in sweat as Derrick slowly pulled out of Stephanie. He gently massaged her back for a minute before reaching up to untie her.

"I'll get the shower started," he said as he kissed the back of her neck while undoing her restraints.

"Are we even now, Mister?" Stephanie asked with a sassy tone.

"We are very even now," Derrick said between deep breaths. "Now, let's get in the shower so I can clean you up and get you home."

"Kicking me out, are you?"

Derrick replied, "I just assumed you'd have to leave."

Stephanie rolled into Derrick's arms, which wrapped around her, and she said, "I'm not going anywhere tonight."

"Did you bring clothes to wear tomorrow?"

"Nope, and I really don't care," Stephanie said with a complete sense of contentment.

After their shower, Derrick held Stephanie in his arms as the two started to drift off to sleep between kisses. "I'll never walk away from you again, Derrick," Stephanie said as she went to sleep.

Derrick simply replied, "I know."

● ● ●

Stephanie got to the Suffolk County Courthouse just a few minutes before her hearing was scheduled to begin. She hurried past the security check at the entrance and ran through the lobby, racing to reach the courtroom on time. As she was running, Stephanie dug her hand into her purse and retrieved her phone. She powered it up for the first time since she left for work the night before, and it began vibrating non-stop with an onslaught of incoming text messages and voicemail notifications.

"Oh shit, oh shit," Stephanie said as she scrolled through text after text from Jacob and Bill Webber demanding to know where she was.

Stephanie walked briskly down the long hallway leading to the courtroom, and she saw Webber standing at the end of the hallway. Webber started walking towards her until they met in the middle. Stephanie stood before him with her hair barely brushed, and her makeup was just a shadowed remnant of what she had applied the day before. Having stayed at Derrick's place unexpectedly left Stephanie completely unprepared.

"I very rarely get angry, Bradford, and I very rarely lose my cool, but I am one step away from completely losing it right now. Where the hell have you been?"

Stephanie's eyes began to well up as she answered, "Sir, I'm so sorry. I was feeling sick again last night and..."

Webber interrupted, "Stop! Just stop! You disappeared from work yesterday without saying a word to anyone, you completely blew off our preparation meeting, and you don't answer your phone or text me back? And to top it off, you're wearing the same clothes as yesterday. I don't know what the hell is going on in your life, but you better pull it together, Bradford."

"I will Mr. Webber; I will. Can we go in so we can get the hearing started?"

"You're kidding me right? Number one, there's no way you're going in front of a judge looking like that; you're not going to embarrass my office like that. And number two, we can't go into a hearing if the prosecuting attorney doesn't show up for the preparation meeting the night before. So no, Bradford, we can't go in and get started. I talked to the judge and he postponed the hearing until next week."

Tears began streaming down Stephanie's face as she told Webber, "This will never, ever happen again. I promise you."

"I know it won't, because you're not the lead on this anymore; I'm handing it off. And if you ever put me in a position like this again, you'll be out on your ass." Webber started to walk away but suddenly stopped and looked back to Stephanie, "Oh and one more thing. You better think of something a hell of a lot better than saying you're sick when you get home."

"What?" Stephanie asked.

"Your husband was calling me every fifteen minutes until he finally stopped at three in the morning. I'd come up with something good if I were you."

Stephanie cried in her car for over an hour before she finally placed the gear selector in drive and started driving home. Stephanie's emotions shifted back and forth between the pure terror of facing Jacob and feelings of just not caring anymore. By the time Stephanie's foot crossed the threshold of her front door, she just didn't give a shit about what Jacob thought.

Stephanie walked passed through the living room, as if nothing had happened, until Jacob stopped her.

"Whoa, whoa, whoa...where are you going?" He asked.

"To bed. I'm tired."

"You're tired? You're out all night without a phone call or anything, and all you have to say is that you're tired?"

"What do you want from me, Jacob? I'm going to bed," Stephanie said as she was raising her phone to check her text messages.

Jacob grabbed the phone from Stephanie's hand, and smashing it to pieces by throwing it against the wall. Jacob screamed, "I want to know where the hell you were last night. I want to know who he is!"

"You want to know who who is?" Stephanie asked in a very condescending tone.

"The man you were with last night."

"You're such an asshole, Jacob. I was with Karen. I thought your overnight flight was last night, and I went to Karen's for drinks, and my phone died." Stephanie sharply retorted.

"If you were with Karen, why wouldn't you answer your phone?"

"Because my phone died, and I didn't want to drive home after having drinks."

"That's bullshit Stephanie, and you know it! You always text me saying you love me before I go for a flight, and I didn't hear shit from you. You knew my overnight wasn't until tonight. And you didn't even show up for your meeting last night at work; I had your boss calling me looking for you. So, stop lying to me."

"Fine, I knew you were home. I stayed at Karen's because I didn't want to come home, and I didn't want to talk to you. You're the reason I didn't want to come home, so why on Earth would I want to talk to you?"

"What the hell did I do to make you not want to come home?"

"It's not what you did, it's what you don't do, what you won't do, and what you'll never do," Stephanie said as she grew angrier.

Jacob exploded again, "What the fuck are you talking about?"

"Wake the fuck up, Jacob. I parade around here every night after work in these skirts, heels, lingerie, and anything else I can come up with to get your attention. And you know what I get? Nothing. Not one god damned thing!"

"Where is this coming from?"

"It's coming from me being sick and tired of begging and pleading for you to actually notice me and actually want to fuck me."

Jacob reminded Stephanie, "We just had sex last weekend."

"Yes, Jacob, we had sex. We had sex, and I'm begging you to fuck me, and not just climb on until you cum and then roll over to call it quits."

"What do you want that I'm not doing?"

"Be a man! Manhandle me, be rough with me, pull my hair, and spank me. Make me do things I don't want to do," blurted Stephanie.

"What? You're my wife, not some god damned whore!"

"Maybe I want to be your wife and your whore," Stephanie cried out. "In that bedroom, treat me like your fucking whore. My god, how many guys would kill to have me say that to them, and here I am, just offering it to you. What do I get in return? You look at me like I'm the crazy one."

"This is insane. I think you're losing your fucking mind."

"Whatever, Jacob," Stephanie said as she started walking away. "Either start acting like a man with me, or I'll find someone who will."

"Don't walk away from me," Jacob yelled.

Jacob yelled again, but his demand fell on deaf ears as Stephanie slammed the bedroom door behind her. Jacob drew back his arm and punched the wall as he yelled, "What the fuck!"

• • •

Just a few hours later, Jacob was behind the controls of the 737 airliner as it began to turn onto the runway. He pushed the accelerator levers forward, the jets roared to life, and the plane began to hurtle the passengers faster and faster.

Jacob and his co-pilot ran through the checklists until Jacob pulled back on the yoke, and the nose rotated up toward the sky. The cockpit was filled with chatter between the two pilots and the air traffic controllers, as they passed through ten thousand feet, and Jacob began a conversation with his co-pilot as he set the autopilot adjustments for the flight.

"I think she's cheating on me, Mark," Jacob said.

"What? Say that again," Mark said with a stunned tone.

"My wife, I think she's cheating on me."

"Stephanie? No way, man. Stephanie loves you," Mark tried to reassure Jacob.

"I'm telling you, she is."

"What makes you think that?"

"She's been acting so strange lately. She's just different, and she's so distant."

Mark offered, "Maybe she's just going through something. My wife goes through these little funks all the time. Try to do something nice for her; something to get her mind off of things."

"But there's more. She's been so protective of her phone lately. She's always either on it, or she hides it. She never just leaves it laying around, and she'll never use it in front of me. She tells me she's texting her friend from work, but she just goes about it so weird."

"Check your account online, and you can see who she's talking to," said Mark.

"Which brings up another strike: she changed our account plan so our statements are separate now. She thinks I didn't notice, but she did that right around the same time this all started."

"That is definitely strange," Mark agreed.

"But the worst part is, she never came home from work last night. Then she strolled in this morning acting like everything was cool as can be."

"What?" asked Mark with disbelief. "Where did she say she was?"

"Her friend from work again. But, Mark, I know it was bullshit. When she got home, there wasn't an ounce of her being sorry or her trying to explain. She just tried turning it around on me by starting a fight and making me out to be the bad guy."

"What does her turning it around on you prove?"

"That she has something to hide. If she was telling the truth, she'd be sorry about it, but by turning it around on me and starting a different fight, she pulled the attention away from her not coming home. She was with another man."

"So, what are you going to do about it?" Mark asked.

"I'm going to confront her about everything and make her tell me the truth. Then I'll deal with it from there."

"Look, I don't want to put my nose where it doesn't belong, but you need to get real."

"Get?" Jacob asked.

Mark said, "You're going to confront her, and you honestly think she's just going to fess up to something? And then, even if she does, what are you planning on doing?"

"I'll walk away," Jacob said. "I'm not staying in my marriage if she's cheating on me. I won't do it."

"Because it's that simple, right? You can just walk away? How much do you have to lose by this?" Mark asked.

"Well, we don't have any kids, so I guess not a lot."

Mark replied, "How about leaving your own house and getting stuck paying half the mortgage? How about paying her half your pension the day you retire? How about alimony?"

"How can she just make me leave the house? That's just as much mine as it is hers."

"Have you ever heard of domestic violence? She calls the police and says you hit her, and that's it, you go."

Offended by Mark's comment, Jacob replied, "Stephanie would never do that."

"Just like she'd never cheat on you right? I bet there was a time you would have said that, too."

"So what do you suggest I do?" Jacob asked after a short pause.

"Get all your ducks in a row," said Mark. "Start transferring money from your accounts into one in your mother or father's name. Build up your own nest egg. Then, understand that once you confront her you're going to have to leave, so have an apartment ready. The day you confront her, rent a truck and take everything you want out of the house before she gets home from work – your T.V., your furniture, everything. And last, before you say one word to her, have proof. Do whatever you have to do, but don't give her any room to lie her way out of it. Know who the other guy is, know where he works, know where he lives, find out if he's married, find out everything."

"I will. Thanks, Mark."

"Jacob, I'm telling you, you better have tangible proof when you confront her. If it's just your suspicion, she's going to take you through the ringer. But if you know every last detail about her and this other guy, she stands to face a lot of embarrassment, and so does he. Who the hell wants everyone knowing they cheated on their spouse and got caught? Avoiding that embarrassment will be exactly what motivates her to want to end things clean, fairly, and quickly."

"Thanks, Mark. Now, let me ask you a question: do you think she's cheating on me?"

"Based on what you told me?" Mark asked.

"Yes, based on what I've told you."

"I hate to say it, buddy, but if you even have to ask, you probably already know the answer."

● ● ●

7
Red Handed

While Jacob was off on his overnight flight, Stephanie found herself home alone and still fuming over her fight with Jacob. She initiated a message with Derrick, **"What'cha doing?"**

"Not much, just thinking of you," Derrick replied.

"Up for doing something?" Stephanie asked.

"I'm always up for something fun. What did you have in mind?"

"Anything involving your motorcycle," answered Stephanie. **"Don't laugh, but I've never been on a bike."**

"You're really starting to make this hard for me to say no."

"And just why would you want to say no, mister?"

Derrick replied, **"Where do you want me to meet you?"**

"Your turn to come to me," she wrote. **"There's a little plaza down the street from my house, and I'll meet you there in one hour."**

Stephanie gave Derrick the directions, and he simply replied, **"On my way."**

An hour later, Derrick roared into the parking lot, unleashing a loud rumble with each flick of his wrist on the throttle. Stephanie watched him pulling in, wearing his tattered jeans, boots, and tight-fitting white T-shirt. His style, his attitude, and his tattooed arms all fit perfectly with his motorcycle, and Stephanie was loving every inch of him. She watched him park his bike, and as he was pulling his phone from his pocket to text her, she stepped out of her car and started walking to him.

Derrick was mid-way through his text when he looked up and saw Stephanie. She was wearing a very tight, form-fitting T-shirt, very short denim shorts, and cork wedge heels. Her adorable outfit and her beautifully tanned skin made Derrick utter, "Girl, I just want to eat you up," as she approached.

"Play your cards right, and you just might," she flirted back. "But just be careful, I'm not as innocent as I look."

Derrick leaned forward, inviting Stephanie to climb onto the back of his bike, and he said, "Let's roll, bad girl."

Stephanie climbed on, and she wrapped her arms around Derrick's waist as he started the engine and brought the thunderous exhaust to life.

"Oh my God, that's loud," Stephanie yelled into Derrick's ear.

"You just hang on," Derrick said before suddenly driving through the parking lot and to the main road.

Derrick drove to the highway where he immediately drifted to the left lane and rapidly accelerated the bike to well over ninety miles per hour. Stephanie let out a thrilled scream as they blew past the slower cars. Stephanie yelled, "Where are we going?" but Derrick only replied by revving the motor and driving even faster.

Derrick drove about forty-five minutes west of Boston, and he exited the highway to a secondary country road. The back road rolled through gentle hills and curves, and the forest on either side of the pavement had grown so tall, a canopy of trees completely covered them. Derrick slowed his speed down, as this wasn't a thrill ride, this was something different. This was an experience to be taken in slowly and not rushed.

Stephanie's arms wrapped tighter around Derrick's waist, and her hands rubbed against his abdomen and chest as she pressed the side of her face against his back. Stephanie closed her eyes as she felt the breeze blowing over her face, and the mixed smell of Derrick's natural odor and the fresh forest air was the most intoxicating aroma she had ever sensed.

As the afternoon was wearing on, the sky began to darken from the clouds rolling in. The air became heavy with the smell of rain as the first sprinkle appeared. Derrick pulled off to the side of the road as the rain grew steadier.

As Derrick turned off the engine, Stephanie asked, "Why are you stopping? It's raining."

"The road's going to be slick. I'm cool with risking it by myself, but not with you."

"But Derrick, we're in the middle of the woods, and it's pouring!"

Derrick got off the motorcycle, and he lifted Stephanie to help her down. "It's okay," he replied. "Follow me."

Derrick took Stephanie by the hand and he ran, pulling her behind him. He found a large tree which was filled with branches and leaves, and he led Stephanie under it.

"It's not the best, but it'll do. It won't rain long," Derrick said.

"It won't be long?" Stephanie asked. "Then I don't want to waste it."

Her long brown hair was dripping, with rain falling down her face to her lips. Derrick's hand grabbed the back of her neck, and pulled her in to kiss her deeply. Derrick stepped forward into Stephanie, causing her to step back until she was pressed against the tree. Derrick's drenched shirt was clinging to his body, and it stuck to him as Stephanie began pulling it off. Derrick pulled Stephanie in close as he was kissing her, and each press of his lips against hers felt like her very first kiss all over again.

Derrick's hands began unbuttoning Stephanie's tiny shorts, and once undone, she couldn't get them off fast enough. As the rain fell on them, Derrick lifted Stephanie off of the ground. She wrapped her legs around him, and with her back pressed against the tree, he made passionate love to her. Stephanie was overcome with emotion since this was so different from her other experiences with Derrick. This was the kind of powerful, connecting, and loving sex Stephanie had always dreamed of having. *I love this man*, she thought to herself but didn't dare have the courage to say out loud.

As the passing rain began to let up, Derrick stopped making love to Stephanie. He kissed her gently and she asked, "You didn't cum. Do you want me to finish you another way?"

Derrick kissed Stephanie and replied, "You didn't either."

"This time, it wasn't about cumming for me," Stephanie replied.

Derrick softly said, "It wasn't for me either."

Derrick and Stephanie dressed themselves and walked back to Derrick's motorcycle, holding hands and laughing. The ride home was bone-chilling as the cool night air rushed against their damp bodies. Stephanie pulled herself in close to Derrick to keep warm, but even the cold chill couldn't dampen her emotions. After spending years with

Jacob, building a life with him, and thinking she knew what love was, Stephanie felt as though she had finally found what love was supposed to feel like.

Knowing Jacob was gone for the night, Stephanie had Derrick drive to her house. Stephanie invited Derrick in to dry his clothes, and he graciously accepted the offer.

"You're sure your husband isn't coming home?" Derrick asked.

"I'm sure."

"One hundred percent sure?" He asked again.

"I promise. He's an airline pilot, and he's on an overnight flight, so it's not like he can just leave work early and come home." explained Stephanie. "What's the matter, is my tough guy suddenly afraid?"

"Shut up, brat," Derrick joked back.

"Besides," continued Stephanie, "even if he did show up, I know you could easily kick his ass."

"That's one lucky guy you have there," Derrick said in jest.

Stephanie put Derrick's clothes in the drier, and he stood in her kitchen wearing only his underwear as Stephanie made coffee. "I feel like an idiot standing here in my underwear, you know!"

"Good, jerk! Now you know how I felt when *you* made me strip in your kitchen." Stephanie wrapped her arms around Derrick and continued, "But you can punish me any time you want. You know I'll do anything for you, right?"

"I do. There is one thing, though, one thing I don't think you'll ever do."

"Ask me. The worst I can say is no," Stephanie said as she turned to finish making coffee.

"It's a little awkward to bring up," said Derrick.

"If it's awkward for you, it's got to be bad – oh God, if you even tell me you want to piss on me, I'll kick your ass!" Stephanie said laughingly.

"I want you...." Derrick said without finishing. "I want you...."

"Come on, goofball, spit it out. You want me to what?"

"Nothing," Derrick said. "There's nothing after it. I just want you."

Stephanie nearly dropped the coffee mug from her hand. Without turning to look at Derrick, she asked, "What are you asking me, Derrick?"

"I want a relationship with you -- a real relationship, but it's never going to work like this. I'm telling you that I'm willing to make the jump, but only if you're in it with me." There was a long pause with no response from Stephanie when Derrick said, "I want you to leave your husband."

• • •

The following day at lunch, Karen shouted "What!?!" when Stephanie told her what Derrick said. "Wait, wait, wait...back up. He asked you to leave Jacob?"

"He actually told me he was falling for me, and he is starting to think he's going to get hurt. Derrick said he's afraid of falling in love with me only to have me leave him and go back to Jacob."

"What did you say? Did you tell him he was crazy?" Karen asked.

"Why would I tell him he's crazy?" Stephanie asked.

"Because, you're not really going to leave Jacob, are you?"

Stephanie said, "I think I am, Karen. I really think I belong with Derrick."

"Are you kidding me right now?" Karen asked, almost angry by the thought of Stephanie leaving her husband.

"What the hell is your problem?" Stephanie lashed out.

"I just don't see why he needs to rush you into leaving Jacob."

"Derrick isn't rushing me into anything. He told me how he feels, and I feel the exact same way."

Karen asked, "But why does he want you to leave your husband all of a sudden? You barely even know this guy, Stephanie! Have you lost your mind?"

"Because he said he's been hurt bad in the past, he's afraid, and no, I haven't lost my mind," explained Stephanie.

"Afraid? I think he's full of shit," Karen said without reason.

"Karen, what the fuck? This is why I hate talking to you about this -- you're so wishy-washy. One day you think he's bad for me, then you think he's good, then I need to run from him, then you want me to go back to him, and now he's a liar? You don't even know him."

"I know him better than you think," Karen said.

"And what's that supposed to mean?" Stephanie asked.

"I know his kind. I'm telling you Stephanie, this guy's trouble!" said Karen as she got up, walked away from the table and stormed out of the restaurant.

Stephanie, completely confused and irritated by the conversation, had no idea what had just happened. It was at the same exact table where Karen had recently told Stephanie to go back to Derrick and see where this could lead. It was there that Karen suggested perhaps Derrick was the right person for her. Now, however, Karen had completely changed, and Stephanie was at a total loss for any understanding of why.

● ● ●

Stephanie arrived home, and Jacob was already there. She walked through the house without even acknowledging him, and Jacob returned in kind. Stephanie saw an empty pizza box on the counter, and since she was hungry, she asked, "Did you save me any?"

Jacob coldly answered, "Why would I?" without even turning from the television.

"Whatever, asshole."

"Yeah, Stephanie, I'm the asshole."

Stephanie said, "Don't even talk to me." A moment later she continued, "When's your next overnight?"

Jacob replied, "Why so you can go fuck your boyfriend again?" without even thinking of his conversation with Mark. As soon as the words rolled from his tongue, Jacob cringed with regret.

"No, so I can have Karen over for a girls' night," Stephanie said. "You disgust me."

Jacob struggled not to argue back. He knew Stephanie was lying, and he wanted to challenge her on her lie, but he knew his friend was right. Jacob knew he didn't have the ammunition to win this war, and accordingly, he backed down.

"I'm sorry," Jacob said with enormous restraint. "That was wrong of me to accuse you of something like that. You've never done anything to come even close to deserving this." Jacob forced himself to continue, "I'll be gone on Tuesday night next week."

Stephanie retrieved a frozen dinner from the freezer and counted down the minutes on the microwave until her meal was ready. She couldn't even stand to be in the same room as Jacob anymore, but she couldn't understand why. Stephanie knew she was the one who was betraying her husband, she knew she was the one who was violating her marriage, and she knew Jacob had never done anything even close to the sort; however, she couldn't get beyond her feeling that she couldn't stomach to be around him. The simple fact was every minute Stephanie was around Jacob, she wasn't with Derrick, and she blamed Jacob for standing in her way. As Stephanie's resentment towards Jacob grew, his own confusion of the situation multiplied, and Jacob had no idea what he had done wrong.

Stephanie finished her dinner, and she got ready for bed. Jacob was still on the living room couch when he heard Stephanie close the door to the spare bedroom. Stephanie had moved most of her things to the spare room, and she had stopped sleeping with Jacob. Their relationship had eroded from a marriage to being mere roommates. Stephanie was the love of Jacob's life, and as he watched what was happening, his heart crushed. For the first time in Jacob's adult life, he cried. Jacob had no clue where to turn next, and he decided to begin taking steps to protect himself. Jacob was ready to follow Mark's advice.

• • •

When the following Tuesday morning finally arrived, Jacob stayed in bed while he listened to Stephanie leaving for work. Once he was certain she was gone, he got out of bed and prepared his day. He drove his car towards a local shopping center as he dialed his cell phone.

"Hello, this is Jacob Bradford. I'm scheduled to fly flight 513, scheduled for a four o'clock departure, this afternoon." There was a short pause, as the person on the other end spoke, before Jacob continued, "I'm feeling terrible today, and it won't be safe for me to fly tonight. I'm going to need to stay home sick."

Jacob arrived at the store and began walking aisle to aisle, and he placed a list of items into his shopping cart. Jacob selected binoculars, a baseball cap, sunglasses, a digital voice recorder, a note pad, paper towels and glass cleaner. Jacob then went to the electronics department and began browsing video camcorders.

"Is there anything I can help you with, sir?" a young sales associate asked.

"Are you familiar with the video recorders?" Jacob asked in reply.

"I know them pretty well. What are you looking for?"

Jacob said, "I need one that has a very powerful zoom. I need to be able to see really excellent detail from a pretty good distance."

"I know exactly what you're looking for. It's right over here," the salesman said while pointing to the cameras on the other side of the display. "This one right here has the best zoom, and the video quality, even at full zoom, is pretty awesome."

"This is over a thousand dollars!"

"If you want the best one we have, it's not going to be cheap. We have other digital camcorders for under a few hundred, but the quality isn't going to be there."

"No, this is the one I need. If I get this, can you ring up everything here?"

"I sure can," said the salesman.

Jacob left the store, and he made a beeline for the airport where he was originally scheduled to depart that afternoon. He followed the signs for long-term parking, and he drove through the parking garage until he found a spot. Jacob left his car and walked nearly a mile, along the busy airport roadway, to the car rental section of the airport. Jacob rented a very plain, run-of-the-mill sedan that would easily blend in with other cars.

Jacob sat in the rental car before leaving the lot, and he used his phone to look for a car shop that did window tinting. Jacob went to the shop and got the cheapest tint available. The window tint technician tried, without success, to get Jacob to upgrade to a higher quality tint.

"You know, the cheapest tint isn't going to last very long. The edges are going to peel, and the tinting will actually fade over time," the technician explained.

Jacob asked, "Will it last until tomorrow?"

Confused, the employee answered, "Yeah, it will last until tomorrow."

"Then that's all I need," Jacob answered. "I just need it for tonight, then I'm peeling it off."

The employee asked, "Is this your car?" as he glanced at Jacob's rental.

"If I wanted someone to give me a hard time, I'd just go call my wife. So, how about you just put the tint on the car like I'm paying you to do."

Slightly intimidated by the situation, the employee agreed and applied the darkest tint the shop offered. An hour later, Jacob was impressed with the job when he saw that he couldn't see inside the vehicle at all.

Jacob drove to the parking garage in Boston where he knew Stephanie parked every day. He drove through the garage until he found her car. Knowing for certain her car was in the garage, Jacob exited the garage and found street parking where he could see the exit from the garage, and he just waited. At four o'clock, Jacob sent Stephanie a text message, **"I know we're fighting, but we're getting ready to take off, and I do love you."**

As Jacob finished the text and hit send, he looked up and saw Stephanie walk directly past his rental. Between the tinted windows and the unfamiliar vehicle, Stephanie didn't notice a thing. Stephanie pulled her phone from her purse and glanced at it, but she quickly returned the phone without sending a reply. Jacob knew she just saw his text and couldn't even be bothered to say anything back to him. With that single act, Jacob's hurt was beginning to turn to anger.

Stephanie walked into the pedestrian entrance to the garage, and a few minutes later, her car pulled out of the exit. Jacob followed her while being cautious to not get too close. He stayed behind her until she parked along the north side of Boston Common, Boston's largest public park. Jacob continued to drive until he found another open parking spot, but by the time he had, he lost Stephanie.

"Shit! Shit! Shit!" Jacob yelled while desperately swiveling his head trying to find where Stephanie went.

Jacob was parked with Boston Common to his left and a coffee shop directly to his right. He continued to look around, starting to think he blew it, when he suddenly saw Stephanie walking by his car again, and she entered the coffee shop directly next to him. *Here we go,* Jacob thought.

Jacob prepared the video recorder, and began recording the door to the coffee shop. He had no idea how long Stephanie would be in the shop, but he didn't want to risk missing the chance to record her with whoever she was there to meet. Jacob didn't need to wait long, and within a few moments, Stephanie emerged, hand-and-hand with Derrick. Jacob fought every urge in his body to confront the two, and he knew he needed to be fully prepared before he ended his marriage. This was only the first step, and Jacob continued to record Stephanie and Derrick as they walked to Derrick's apartment building and through the front door. Jacob saw Stephanie was carrying her purse as well as an overnight bag, and he prepared himself for the thought that Stephanie may be spending the night with this man.

Jacob checked his phone frequently over the next several hours, hoping Stephanie would respond to his earlier text, but he received nothing. Just after eleven-thirty, and about seven hours after she had gone into the apartment building, Jacob saw Stephanie emerge with Derrick. Jacob fumbled to get the video recorder, and he pressed the red record button just in time to capture Derrick and Stephanie holding one another while they kissed goodnight. Jacob zoomed in to capture the detail of the embrace between his wife and this other man, and his stomach churned with pain as he recorded each second.

The lovers parted ways, with Stephanie walking towards her car and Derrick going back inside. Jacob noticed Stephanie was no longer wearing her work attire, and she was now wearing tight, black yoga pants, a cute T-shirt, and sneakers. His imagination wandered relentlessly as he struggled to avoid thinking of what she could have been doing in the apartment.

Jacob saw Stephanie's car drive by his rental, and he was preparing to follow her to see where she went next. Jacob waited for a few moments before pulling out of his parking spot to avoid being directly behind her. As Jacob was preparing to drive, he saw Derrick emerge from the building and walking toward the coffee shop.

"Where's he going?" Jacob wondered, as his plan suddenly shifted.

Jacob exited the vehicle and began following Derrick on foot. Jacob worked to stay close enough to Derrick to keep constant view of him but far enough to avoid detection. Fortunately for Jacob, Derrick's journey was short, and he entered a nearby bar.

Jacob stood by the entrance to the bar, taking a few deep breaths in an attempt to maintain his composure. Having no idea what he was going to do next, Jacob pulled open the door to the bar and walked in. He saw Derrick sitting at the bar, and Jacob sat on the only remaining empty stool, right next to Derrick.

As Jacob sat at the bar, Derrick being Derrick looked to him and said, "Listen buddy, you keep your hands to yourself, I'll keep my hands to myself, and we'll get along just fine."

"What?" Jacob, thinking he was caught, nervously asked.

"I'm kidding, brother," said Derrick. "I'm just kidding."

"Oh," Jacob nervously continued, "It's okay."

"I'm sorry, man. Let me get you a drink," Derrick offered while having no idea why he made the man he was talking to so nervous. "What do you want?"

Jacob, realizing he was being faced with the best opportunity he could ask for, said, "No, I'm sorry. I've just had a tough day. I'd love a vodka-cranberry."

"Vodka-cranberry?" Derrick asked. He jokingly continued, "That's what my grandmother drinks, but to each his own. Bartender, a vodka-cranberry for my new friend, and whiskey neat for me."

"You got it, guys," the bartender replied as Derrick stuck his hand out to Jacob.

"I'm Anthony," said Derrick, giving a fake name out of suspicion of the stranger sitting next to him.

Jacob, having no idea that Stephanie knew this man as "Derrick," saw nothing unusual and shook his hand. Jacob was uncertain how much Derrick actually knew of him, and he had to give a false name.

"I'm Steve," said Jacob.

"Cool to meet you, buddy," Derrick said.

With the exception of the complete change of names, the two had an otherwise normal conversation. Derrick rarely sat alone for long before making a new friend, and this was no exception. The only difference this time being that Derrick's new friend was faking every smile, and he was actually fighting the enormous temptation to kill Derrick.

"What are you doing here, tonight?" Derrick asked.

Jacob waved his left hand, showing his wedding band, and said, "Wife's pissing me off, so I needed to get out for a little bit."

Derrick laughed and said, "Out looking for a little strange, huh?"

"A little strange?" Jacob asked.

"Some strange ass," Derrick said. He explained further, "Looking for a girl."

"No, I'm not looking," Jacob answered.

"But if the opportunity knocked, you wouldn't answer?"

Jacob forced a fake laugh and said, "Now, I never said that! But what about you, you married?"

"No way, brother. You were crazy enough to make that mistake, not me."

"You're telling me, man. No girlfriend or anything?" Jacob asked.

"I wouldn't call them girlfriends, but I have my fingers in a few little honeypots, if you know what I mean."

"No shit? You can't leave it at that; I need to vicariously live through you for a minute," said Jacob.

"I just have two stringing along right now. One is a little blonde that I've been tapping for a while, and she's starting to get a little on the boring side - kind of reached my end with her. But my most recent one, is a tight little brunette that's a shit ton of fun."

"Man, I wish I wasn't married," Jacob announced.

"What difference does it make? This brunette is married, and she doesn't seem to give a shit. Why should you?"

"One of your girls is married?" Jacob asked.

"Actually, they're both married. But the blonde, I've already run through her, and it's getting old. I'm just getting this new one broken-in, and that's the fun part," Derrick told Jacob.

Jacob squeezed his glass tight, and he could feel his face getting red as anger and hatred consumed his body. Jacob's discipline prevailed, however, and he replied, "Broken in? Now this you have to explain to me," with yet another forced laugh.

"Yeah, breaking her in. She's that good-girl type that's really a little freak dying to break out. She just needed someone to get her inner freak to come out and play, and brother, I was more than happy to oblige."

"I need to get myself something like that," Jacob said to maintain the facade. "What kind of stuff do you have this girl doing?"

"Name it, man - damn near anything you can think of. This one is straight up down for anything. I just had her over at my place earlier tonight, and I had her doing some fucked up shit. I'm telling you, bro, she eats this shit up. I could probably tell her I wanted to piss on her, and her only reaction would be begging me for more."

"How the hell do you get them to turn like that?" Jacob questioned Derrick.

"I have some tricks, brother, but basically just treat a slut like a lady and treat a lady like a slut, and they'll love it. If she's a nice girl, the kind that always does the right thing, treat her like a whore and she'll love it. Don't ask me why, just is what it is."

"And that's all there is to it?" asked Jacob.

"Well, not always. With this new one, the brunette, I have a secret weapon. I have something that gives me…I'll just say an unfair advantage," Derrick said. He continued, "And on that, it's time for me to roll, Steve."

"Yeah, I need to get home, too. Cool meeting you, Anthony."

Derrick threw a few twenty-dollar bills on the bar as he said, "That should take care of everything." Derrick patted Jacob on the back and finished with, "Now go find yourself some fun, buddy," as he walked away.

Jacob, completely filled with rage, watched Derrick walk through the door and out of the bar. Jacob reached into his shirt pocket and pulled out the small digital voice recorder he bought earlier in the day. The device made a small beep as he pressed the stop button. Jacob walked back to his rental car, and once inside, he pressed play on the voice recorder. Jacob heard Derrick's voice emanating from the device:

Listen buddy, you keep your hands to yourself, I'll keep my hands to myself, and we'll get along just fine…

I got you, you fucker! Jacob thought as he stopped playing the recording. *I so got you!*

Jacob drove to the airport, and stopped in a nearby parking lot to remove the tint from the windows. He used the paper towels and glass cleaner to return the glass to its original state as it was when he rented the car. Jacob returned the rental and walked back to his own vehicle in the long-term parking garage. Jacob looked at the clock on the car dash and saw it was nearly five o'clock in the morning. Completely exhausted, Jacob just reclined the front seat and fell asleep in his car.

• • •

8

A Night to Forget

Jacob spent the better part of the next two weeks preparing for his inevitable confrontation with Stephanie. He had the video of Stephanie with Derrick, he had the recording of his conversation with Derrick, and there was no room for Stephanie to wiggle her way out of accepting responsibility for what she was doing. Jacob also knew Derrick's derogatory description of his relationship with Stephanie would only further encourage her to be willing to end the marriage quietly – otherwise could prove humiliating for her.

Ten days after he recorded Derrick, Jacob was in the cockpit with Mark once again. After leveling off at thirty-seven thousand feet, Mark cautiously asked, "So, how's everything going?"

Jacob, wearing his white, short-sleeve, button down shirt with pilot lapels, slid his pilot headset from his ears. The headset ruffled his short, brown hair, and he paused before answering, "I'm not sure if the answer is good or bad." He continued, "It's bad in that I confirmed everything, and she is cheating. It's good, though, in that I have everything I need to make sure she doesn't rake me over the coals in a divorce."

"I'm sorry to hear that, but I'm glad you at least have something to protect yourself," Mark said as the cockpit bounced from a light patch of turbulence.

"Thanks to you. If it wasn't for what you told me, I would have run in like an idiot and been left with nothing."

"What steps are you taking before you walk out?" Mark asked.

"I'm being fair with her. I opened up a new bank account, at a different bank and in just my name, and I'm just going to transfer half of all our savings to it. I also signed a lease on an apartment, and I'm only going to take what I absolutely need from the house. I'll leave her with half the savings and most of the stuff in the house. Then when it's time to discuss the house, I'll be open. If she wants to keep the house for herself, she can have it. If she wants to sell it and split the equity fifty-fifty, then I'm okay with that, too. I think I'll come out of this pretty clean."

"Sounds like you have it all worked out," Mark said approvingly. "When are you pulling the trigger?"

"She thinks my next overnight flight is next Tuesday – I told her that, today. I know she'll stay out Tuesday night and not come home until Wednesday after work. That gives me all Tuesday and most of Wednesday to transfer the money from one bank to the other and get everything moved out of the house."

"You need any help moving?" offered Mark.

"No, but thanks anyway. This is going to be really tough for me, and I think I need to do it alone. I know I may look like I'm holding it together pretty well, but I think I'm still in shock. Once the reality of this sets in, I'm going to fall apart. I think I need to be alone when that happens."

"Just let me know if you change your mind. Do you know what you're going to say to her?"

"I'll be there when she comes home on Wednesday – I'll be there waiting. I'm not sure what I'm going to say, but it will be short and to the point. The only thing I need to figure out is how I'm going to get her car."

"Why do you want her car?" Mark asked perplexed.

"Both of the cars are in my name to keep the insurance cheaper, since someone has a problem with the speed limit. My car is paid off, and I don't give a shit what she does with it, but her car still has a loan on it. The car and the loan are in my name, and if she stops paying on it, it's me that will take the hit. I trust that she'll pay on it, but I'm not taking any chances with it. So, on the way out the door, I'm taking her car and she can have mine."

"I know this is going to sound like a complete contradiction from what I said before, but just be cautious not to be too vindictive," warned Mark.

"Do you think I am? I kind of feel like I'm being pretty fair," said Jacob.

Mark replied, "No, I think you're being extremely fair, but just keep it that way. Take it from someone who's been there, this may get painful and hurtful for you, and you might want to lash out and become cruel. But someday, this will all be over. When you look back, you'll want to know that you were the bigger person, and you didn't stoop to a lower level."

"I hear you, and I think I am."

Mark continued, "You're the man in this situation, so don't forget to always act like a man."

Jacob thought about what Mark just said, and he replied, "You're right. That's why I came to you with this – I knew I could trust you to give the best advice." Jacob smiled and changed the topic, "Now level off at thirty-seven thousand feet, and maintain a heading of zero eight six degrees at four hundred twenty knots."

"Flight level three seven zero, heading zero eight six, and four two zero knots," Mark replied as he adjusted the aircraft's auto-pilot settings, and the two flew their passengers into the heavenly blue sky.

● ● ●

The following Monday night eventually arrived, but the days and nights until then were filled with awkwardness between Stephanie and Jacob. The silence in their home was deafening while neither said barely a word to the other. On Tuesday night, Stephanie broke their silence.

"Tomorrow is your overnight flight?" she asked from the living room.

Jacob, who was making a sandwich, replied, "Yeah, I'll be gone until Wednesday morning."

"I'm going to stay over at Karen's tomorrow night. I don't feel like being alone in the house."

Jacob, knowing this was all about to become very real, replied, "Okay, have fun." The words were there, but the tear building in his eye showed he was reaching the limit of what he could endure.

Stephanie was curled up on the couch. Her hair was pulled back in a ponytail, and she was wearing black workout shorts and a tank top. With her phone in her right hand and the television remote in her left, she began a text message with Derrick.

"Guess who!" she typed.

"My bad little princess?" Derrick quickly responded.

"Care for some company tomorrow night?" asked Stephanie.

"I do, but I'm in the mood to go out," said Derrick.

Stephanie asked, **"Dinner?"**

"No," replied Derrick, "Let's go have fun. My buddy's band is playing tomorrow night at a bar over by Boylston Street. I want to go check them out."

"Okay, but only if you promise me we won't be out too late. I absolutely have to be at work on Wednesday, okay?"

Without a second thought, Derrick replied, "Pinky promise! But I have a request of you..."

"Anything for my sexy man," said Stephanie.

"They're an AC/DC cover band, and a lot of the people will dress up in school uniforms like the band did back in the eighties. I know a lot of girls go to their shows in schoolgirl outfits, and I'd love to have my own little schoolgirl there."

"I have the perfect thing in my closet from Halloween," Stephanie told Derrick. "This will be so much fun!"

● ● ●

The following morning, Stephanie packed her bag while Jacob slept. She dug through her closet until she found all the pieces of her outfit, and as she placed each item in her bag, she knew Derrick was going to love what he saw. Stephanie was uneasy about the idea of wearing a naughty schoolgirl outfit to a bar when it was nowhere near Halloween, but if Derrick was so willing to have that kind of fun with her, there was no way she was going to turn him down. Stephanie hadn't done anything like this in years.

Stephanie got to work and sat at her desk when she saw a post-it note stuck to her computer monitor: "My office the second you get in!"

The handwriting was unmistakably Bill Webber's, and Stephanie went to his office as the note instructed. "You wanted to see me, sir?"

"Bradford, this close, I'm this close," Webber said as he made a motion with his thumb and index finger barely spread apart.

"This close to what?" Stephanie asked.

"This close to pulling you entirely off the Hutchinson case. What the hell is going on with you?"

"Did I do something wrong, Bill?" Stephanie asked.

Webber opened a manila folder with the printouts of three emails. He held the printouts in his hand as he said, "Bradford, you were asked three times, three god damned times, to prepare the discovery files to send to Hutchinson's defense attorneys. They were due yesterday. So, is there any reason why I have a voicemail waiting for me this morning saying they never got them?"

"Oh no, oh no, oh no!" Stephanie exclaimed as fear rushed over her. "I forgot to send out the discovery files. I'll go do it right now."

"Don't bother!" Webber declared. "I've got the interns working on it, and they're almost done. And I called the defense attorney and I made up some garbage about there being an error with arranging the courier. I'm getting tired of making excuses for you, Bradford."

"I'm so sorry, Mr. Webber. I just have so much going..." Stephanie started to explain before she was interrupted.

"Stop, just stop. It's been nothing but excuse after excuse over the past few months, and to be honest, I don't care what's going on in your personal life. I don't show up in your kitchen at nine o'clock at night, so don't bring your home life with you to work. One more time, Bradford, and I promise you, you'll be doing nothing but misdemeanors again." Stephanie apologized again, until Webber replied, "No Bradford, I'm sorry I trusted you with this."

Stephanie left Bill Webber's office and went to the conference room to join in the meeting which was set to begin at any moment. As she walked in, she could feel the gaze of everyone falling on her, and it was a feeling of being not wanted.

"Since Stephanie Bradford decided to show up, it looks like we can get started," said Kevin, the attractive, young attorney who had taken over as the lead prosecutor on the Hutchinson case.

The room filled with the shock as Stephanie replied, "Fuck you, Kevin," and walked out of the meeting.

Karen, who was also in the meeting, chased Stephanie into the hallway and asked, "Steph, what the hell? What are you doing?"

Stephanie stood in the hallway, wearing a silk white blouse under a black suit jacket, a black skirt with black heels. She answered, "I'm not listening to that. If no one wants me in there, that's fine, but he doesn't need to be an asshole about it. And you don't have to sit there and just watch."

"I don't have to sit there and watch? You want me to start fighting with my co-workers because you can't keep it together long enough to get through one case? Trust me, I understand this new-love thing you're going through, but it's no excuse to let your work go to shit. Whatever you do, is because you choose to do it, so don't go blaming that on me." Karen paused and ended with, "It's your career, throw it away if you want."

Stephanie walked away, and didn't go back to the meeting. Instead, she walked out of work all together. She clutched her purse in her left hand as her right hand feverishly texted Derrick, "**I need you to take my mind off of the world today**."

She walked to her car, holding her phone and waiting for Derrick's response. She reached her car, and not hearing back yet, she thought *not today Derrick, please not today*.

"**Taking your mind off the world is my specialty**," Derrick replied as Stephanie was sitting in the driver's seat of her car. "**What were you in the mood for**?"

"**Anything to make me smile**," she answered.

Stephanie met Derrick about an hour later at the entrance to the Franklin Park Zoo. She shouted, "This is the best idea ever," as she wrapped her arms around him.

Stephanie looked oddly out of place, walking through the zoo in her business attire, but she didn't care. In fact, she didn't have a care in the world while her hand was in Derrick's and the two walked together talking about Stephanie's worries.

They stopped in front of the orangutan exhibit, and they watched the apes play. A large male sat behind a younger female, grooming her burnt red hair, and picking bugs from her. The male groomed and petted the female, and Stephanie said, "They're just amazing. They're so much like us, but their lives are so much simpler."

"They live in a glass cage," Derrick sarcastically replied. "How much more simple can you get?"

"Look at them, they're just so happy. Why do our lives need to be so complicated?"

He answered, "Because we choose to make them complicated. People are never happy with what they have – we always want more and more. In some ways, it's good. It keeps us moving forward and makes us want to improve our lives. We just need to learn when to stop and realize when we have enough." He gently squeezed Stephanie's hand and said, "We need to realize when we have what we really need to make us happy."

"Are you falling in love with me, Derrick?"

Derrick stared Stephanie directly in her beautiful brown eyes as he replied, "I'm trying not to. God knows, I'm trying not to. But yes, more and more every day."

"Why are you trying not to?" she asked.

"You know why."

"No, I honestly don't," she said.

"You're married, Stephanie."

"I know, Derrick. Please don't let that change the way you feel about me. I'm trying to figure out what to do. I really am."

"Are you getting any closer to knowing?"

"I am. I so am," she said as she gently squeezed his hand back and smiled.

Stephanie and Derrick walked hand-in-hand through the rest of the park, and by the end, Stephanie had forgotten everything. Derrick had a magic about him that made Stephanie feel safe, and her worries, fears, and even her cares always melted away while she was with him.

Derrick walked Stephanie back to her car and said, "Meet me at my place at five?"

"Where are you going until then?"

"I have to stop by work for a little bit. I just have a few things I need to get done, and then I'll meet you at the coffee shop when I get home."

She leaned back against her car as the two held one another. "You're absolutely amazing. You know that, right?" she asked.

Derrick gently kissed her lips and answered, "Not even half as amazing as you." He kissed her and said, "See you at five."

Stephanie struggled to pass the time until five o'clock, but as it always does, the time passed, and she saw Derrick walking to the coffee shop to meet her. With her bag slung over her shoulder, Stephanie walked to Derrick. "Ready for a fun night?" he asked her.

"You have no idea!" she said with a gasp of relief. "But remember our promise. I have to leave kind of early. I cannot be late tomorrow. I'm probably in enough trouble at work as it is for leaving today."

"I promise! I promise!" Derrick said, putting his hands up in a joking manner.

Derrick walked Stephanie to his apartment, and he told her, "We need to hurry. The show starts at six, and parking is going to be a bitch over there."

"Why does it start so early?" she asked.

"The bar does mid-week shows a little earlier than on the weekends. I think they try to appeal to the after-work crowd. Now get in there, and get that cute little ass ready."

While Stephanie was in the bathroom, Derrick got changed in his bedroom. He put on his typical deep-v T-shirt with jeans. Derrick's style was simple, but he wore it extremely well. His white tee, worn jeans, and meticulous grooming came together perfectly with his tattooed arms and faint cologne.

Derrick waited patiently until Stephanie finally emerged from the bathroom. She had her hair parted down the middle and split into two perfectly divided pigtails. Her white, low cut, button down shirt barely covered her midriff, and a loose, pink, pleated, plaid skirt fell just above her mid-thigh. Her white stockings came just above her knee, and they were matched with a pair of pink heels.

Derrick looked at her in awe as he asked, "And you just happened to have this laying around your house?"

"A girl needs to be ready for anything," she slyly winked as she answered. "But there's no way we're taking your bike tonight!"

"I'm not eighteen," Derrick laughed. "I do have a car."

"You're not eighteen, huh?" Stephanie asked as she strutted over to Derrick with her heels clicking on the floor with each step. As she reached him, she continued, "Good, because this schoolgirl loves older men."

Derrick's right hand instantly went to the back of her thigh and slid under her skirt. Her left hand quickly pushed downward on his wrist, and she said, "Oh no you don't. That's for later."

They walked to the lobby where Derrick told her to wait. "I'll bring the car around so you don't have to walk down the street in that."

"Such a gentleman," she said as Derrick left to get the car.

A few minutes later, She saw Derrick pull up in a gorgeous, very new, black BMW seven series. "Being a security guard obviously pays very well," She said to Derrick as she walked passed him opening the car door for her.

"I'm not a security guard, I'm a....whatever, just get in, smart ass!"

Stephanie and Derrick arrived at the bar just a few minutes before the band was set to begin, and no sooner had they walked through the door that the drinks started flowing. The houselights came down, the stage lights lit up, and the band started to play. The old-style bar was packed, wall-to-wall, with patrons ready for a fun night, and Stephanie was no exception. She was ready to have fun. To her surprise, there were a number of girls in schoolgirl outfits, and she no longer felt out of place. To the contrary, she was glad Derrick made the suggestion – she felt sexy and fun.

"Woohoo!" Stephanie yelled as the band started playing, and the guitarist belted out the first licks of the strings.

Knowing she had to work in the morning, Stephanie carefully avoided drinking too much. She saw Derrick look around the room and raise his hand to his mouth, sneaking a pill in without anyone noticing. Stephanie pulled in close to Derrick and said, "I want one, too!"

"Why?" he asked. "Just have a few drinks."

"I can't drink too much tonight, I have to work in the morning. One of those will make it more fun for me -- please?" she begged with an exaggerated pouting lower lip.

Derrick dug his hand into his pocket and he then covertly placed two pills in the palm of Stephanie's hand. "Not out here, though, you'll be way too obvious. Go in the bathroom."

"Okay, I'll be right back."

Stephanie walked into the bathroom, with the pills in one hand and her drink in the other. She was planning on waiting for a stall to open up, but she was surprised to see she was the only woman in the bathroom. She quickly placed the pills in her mouth and washed them down with her Sex on the Beach. As she did so, she realized she was not alone.

"Don't bring any treats if you don't have enough to share with the rest of the class," a woman said in an obvious reference to Stephanie's attire.

"Excuse me?" Stephanie said as she turned to the stranger.

Stephanie saw an attractive woman in her late twenties with tanned skin and brown hair with highlights standing before her. She was very petite, at barely more than five feet tall, with a seductively curvy body type. She was wearing dark skinny jeans, cream-colored pumps, and a loose fitting cream sweater top.

"It's okay, I won't tell the teacher," said the woman. "But only if you share."

"I'm not sure what you're talking about," Stephanie nervously said.

"I saw you take a pill, and I'm just wondering if you have any more."

"I don't even know you," said Stephanie.

"I'm Kristin," the woman said. "Now you do know me."

"Who are you here with?" asked Stephanie.

Kristin answered, "Some girls from work, but they're being so lame. What's your name?"

"I'm Stephanie. I'm here with my boyfriend."

"So that explains the schoolgirl look," Kristin joked.

"Yeah, it does. He wanted me to look the part tonight, so I figured *why not?*"

"Very cool! So do you have any more?" Kristin casually asked.

"Any more what?" Stephanie replied.

Kristin looked around secretively and said, "Pills."

"Oh," Stephanie laughed nervously. "That wasn't what it looked like. It's a prescription I take."

"Okay, now I'm just embarrassed," Kristin said with a red glow over her face.

"Don't be," said Stephanie. "Come hang out with us, when you're done, and have a drink. We'll be over by the side bar."

"I'll find you!" Kristin said.

Stephanie returned to Derrick, and the two danced as the band rocked on. Derrick stood behind her, holding her hips with both facing the stage, and she was grinding back into him, teasing him just enough for her to feel him begin to get hard. The Vicodin racing through Stephanie's veins began to take its hold, and she started to feel that elated feeling she was growing to love.

"Hey, girl!" Kristin shouted as she found Stephanie. "Who's this hot guy?"

Stephanie replied, "This is Derrick, and his butt is all mine!"

"I want to dance, so bad!" Kristin announced. "But every time I do, I get swarmed by guys. Come dance with me!"

Stephanie looked to Derrick and asked, "Do you mind if I go dance?"

"I was just about to go grab another drink, so you go right ahead. What do you ladies want to drink?"

Stephanie said she didn't want another drink and Kristin shouted "Rum and cola!" while pulling Stephanie's hand to the dance floor.

The two ran out and started drawing the eyes of every man within sight. A small part of Stephanie loved the

ANTHONY BRYAN

attention, but the larger majority of her couldn't care less as she just wanted to let go and have fun. While she was dancing with Kristin, Stephanie was reminded of her night in Las Vegas, dancing for Jacob and being rejected. She looked to her side and saw Derrick watching her, and she could feel how much Derrick was enjoying watching her dance with Kristin. Knowing Derrick was watching only made Stephanie want to dance more.

As the hour approached ten o'clock, Stephanie told Derrick it was time to leave.

"Oh no, don't leave!" pleaded Kristin.

"I want to stay, I do, but I have work in the morning. Want to exchange numbers?"

"Does a tissue dance if you put a little boogie in it?" Kristin replied with a drunken joke.

The girls exchanged numbers, and Stephanie said, "Text me this weekend. Maybe we can meet up."

"I will," replied Kristin as the two parted ways.

Stephanie and Derrick walked to his car, and he held the passenger side door open for her. As she entered the car, Derrick gave her a light slap on the ass and said, "Get in there, you."

Derrick walked around to the driver side, and once in the car with the door closed, Stephanie said, "Remember the last time we were alone in the car? Get me to your place fast enough, and maybe you can have a little fun with me in my outfit."

Derrick replied, "Make sure that seat belt is nice and tight, because I drive fast."

Stephanie leaned her seat back slightly, and her hands pulled her skirt up to barely reveal her black, silk panties. She slouched in the seat and said, "I'm not sure I can wait that long," as she lightly caressed her fingers across her thigh.

"Holy shit, I need to drive fast," Derrick said as Stephanie's phone alerted to an incoming text.

She checked the phone and saw a text from Kristin. "Please tell me you haven't left yet," Kristin said.

"We're just leaving now. What's wrong." Stephanie replied. She said to Derrick, "Hang on, don't pull out yet."

"Is everything alright?" he asked.

A second text came from Kristin. "I lost my friends, and one of them is my ride. I hate to ask you, but is there any way I can get a ride from you guys? I promise I don't live far."

"Of course," Stephanie replied. "We'll be in a black BMW right out front."

"So much for getting home early," said Derrick after Stephanie explained the situation.

"Are you sure you don't mind giving her a ride?"

"I'm sure. It's kind of a pain in the ass, but I'd feel horrible if something happened to her."

Stephanie saw Kristin exiting the bar, and she reached across Derrick to press on the horn. Kristin looked up and walked toward the car with a smile. She approached the rear driver's side, and a loud clunk sound could be heard as Derrick unlocked the door.

"Thank you so much, you guys!" said Kristin as she closed the door.

Kristin gave Derrick directions to her apartment, and he was relieved it was only a ten-minute drive. Stephanie turned up the radio, and the car drove off with the loud thump of techno music playing inside.

"Thank you again," Kristin said as Derrick parked in front of the multifamily home where Kristin lived. "Do you two want to come up for a few?"

Derrick started to answer that they were in a hurry to get home when Stephanie interrupted, "Let's just run up for a minute. I have to pee so bad."

Derrick parked the car, and the three walked up the flights of stairs to Kristin's third floor apartment. She opened the door to a modest but older apartment with a hodgepodge of mixed furniture and minimal décor.

"It's not much, but it's all mine," Kristin said as they entered her place. She looked to Stephanie and said, "The bathroom is just past the bedroom on the left."

While Stephanie was in the bathroom, Kristin offered Derrick a drink. He replied, "A beer would be perfect."

"What kind?" Kristin asked as she leaned into the refrigerator. As she did, she could feel Derrick staring at her curvy ass being accentuated by her skinny jeans. She responded by only bending further forward.

"Anything cold," he answered without shifting his gaze.

She turned and handed him a bottle of beer, and as he twisted the cap off, she slid one foot from her heels and started to remove the other.

"Leave the heels on," Derrick said with an authoritative yet seductive tone.

"Really?" Kristin asked.

"I like them. Leave them on."

"Okay," she said with a smile as she stepped back into her tall shoes. "You're bad, aren't you?"

"Only time will tell," he answered.

They heard the toilet flush and the faucet running for a moment when Kristin said, "Hold that thought. It's my turn now," as she walked to the bathroom.

Stephanie opened the door and walked past Kristin as she walked into the bathroom. Stephanie went to Derrick in the kitchen and said, "Finish that beer, and then we have to go."

"Before I finish it, I think we have a few seconds alone."

"Oh yeah?" Stephanie asked as she pressed her body against Derrick's. "And just what do you want to do with these few seconds?"

Without saying a word, Derrick answered by wrapping his hands around Stephanie's waist and kissing her. His lips moved away from her own as they glided towards her ear and neck. Derrick's right hand was pulling her in by the small of her back, and his left hand found its way up her skirt. She raised her right leg, and rubbed the inside of her thigh against him as he continued to kiss her neck.

Neither Stephanie nor Derrick heard Kristin exit the bathroom, and they only knew she was there when they heard her heels enter the kitchen. Stephanie quickly pulled her leg down and stepped back from Derrick. Stephanie, obviously embarrassed by being caught, said, "I'm so sorry."

"Why?" Kristin asked as she walked to Stephanie. "Don't let me interrupt."

Stephanie's heart raced as Kristin stood just inches from her, and Kristin's fingers gently grazed Stephanie's barely exposed midriff. She looked at Derrick to see his reaction, and Stephanie saw Derrick calmly watching while resting his beer bottle on the counter. Derrick reached his right hand to Stephanie's lower waist, and he stepped in close to her. She saw his left hand glide across Kristin's lower back, and the three were just inches from one another. Derrick's hands pulled gently on both girls, and they moved in closer to him.

"Where's your bedroom?" Derrick asked while looking at Kristin.

"On the left, just before the bathroom," she said.

"Why don't you go in there and wait for us. We'll follow you in just a minute."

Kristin walked into her room and closed the door behind her. Uncertain if her new friends would be following shortly or if they would be using the opportunity to leave, she started to get ready for them to come in.

Still in the kitchen, Derrick asked, "Do you want to do this?"

"I do and I don't."

"You do *and* don't want to?" Derrick asked in a confused tone.

"I'd be lying if I said that this hasn't always been a fantasy, an intense fantasy, but I'm scared. What if we start and I don't like it?"

"Isn't that what this is all about, living out your fantasies and holding nothing back?" Derrick's hands groped Stephanie's breasts as he said, "I want you to live this one. Live it with me."

"If we start, and I ask you to stop, promise we will?"

"I promise."

"And promise me you won't have sex with her. That's just too much for me to watch."

Derrick sincerely said, "I promise you, I wouldn't do that."

Stephanie thrust her hand into Derrick's pocket and pulled a small plastic bag with three pills. She dropped one into her damp palm, and swallowed it with a gulp from Derrick's beer.

"I'm ready," she said.

Derrick faced Stephanie towards the counter, and he guided her to place her palms flat on the surface. He gently pushed the palm of his hand against her back until she bent forward. From behind, Derrick started rubbing her through her panties, and she started to gently moan. Derrick felt her panties becoming wet, and he said, "How bad do you want this?"

"So bad, baby."

"How bad?" Derrick repeated while rubbing even harder.

"So fucking bad!" Stephanie moaned.

Derrick stood her up and led her to Kristin's bedroom. He opened the door and saw Kristin on the bed. She was now wearing nothing more than a matching white bra and thong and her cream colored heels.

Stephanie looked to Kristin and told her that she didn't want her to have sex with Derrick, and Kristin replied, "It's not him that I want. It's you."

Stephanie faced the bed with Derrick behind her. He began kissing her neck as his fingers unbuttoned her thin, white top. After the final button was opened, he gently pulled her shirt back from her shoulders and over her arms. Kristin watched from the bed as Derrick kissed Stephanie and fondled her body. Still behind her, with her back against his chest, Derrick's left hand gently wrapped around Stephanie's neck as his right hand went back to rubbing her through her panties. Just as Stephanie began to moan, he whispered into her ear, "Climb up onto the bed."

Stephanie climbed onto the bed, and crawled to Kristin. A sense of euphoria rushed through Stephanie's body as her lips met with Kristin's, and she felt Kristin's warm tongue touch her mint Chapstick-flavored lips. Kristin lowered to her back, and Stephanie crawled forward, until she was on top of her. The two continued kissing as their hands wandered around each other's bodies. Stephanie, on her hands and knees over Kristin, felt Kristin's hands on her breasts as she felt Derrick pulling her tiny thong to the side. She kissed Kristin with more passion as she felt Derrick's warm, powerful tongue pressing into her clit.

Stephanie groaned as Derrick's tongue made pass after pass from her clit, over her pussy, and across her ass. She moaned with each lap of his tongue, and Kristin responded by massaging her breasts and nipples with more desire as Stephanie's hand slid down Kristin's stomach and in the front of her white panties. Stephanie's long, brown hair fell to Kristin's face as her fingers began massaging Kristin's bare, shaved pussy.

Kristin pulled down on the straps of her own lace bra, pulling it to reveal her round, large breasts and pink nipples. Stephanie responded by immediately licking and sucking each nipple, and she knew she was turning Kristin on by how wet she could feel her becoming. Kristin used her elbows to lift her back off the mattress. She unclasped her bra, and she then walked her elbows back, inching herself away from Stephanie. Kristin positioned herself so Stephanie's face was directly above her white panties.

Kristin dug her heels into the bed to raise her hips up, and Stephanie slid her panties from her waist, down her legs, and off of her. Stephanie gently kissed the inside of Kristin's soft thighs, and she bashfully lowered her kisses until she heard Kristin begging her for more. Kristin's fingers ran through her hair, and Kristin raised her hips until her warm pussy was at Stephanie's lips. Despite her fears, Stephanie barely hesitated as her tongue took its first gentle lick of Kristin. Stephanie immediately wanted more of Kristin's tangy sweetness, and she began to lick with more and more pressure.

Stephanie realized she had almost completely forgotten about Derrick as she felt him climb on the bed behind her, and she felt his hard cock sliding inside her. Within moments, he was holding her hips and pounding her pussy while Kristin's hot cunt was in her watering mouth. With each powerful thrust from Derrick, Stephanie's face was being pushed into Kristin, and both women were loving it. Without stopping, Stephanie shifted her eyes upwards to see Kristin watching her over her large breasts. Their eyes locked, and Kristin whimpered, "Oh God, eat my pussy!"

Stephanie stayed in her hands-and-knees position, but Kristin adjusted herself so she was now under Stephanie - positioned for both girls to lick each other simultaneously. Stephanie, wearing her plaid skirt, white stockings and pink heels, and Kristin, wearing only her heels and her lowered bra, devoured one another in an erotic sixty-nine position.

Derrick's hard cock began ramming Stephanie, with a force and intensity she had never imagined, while Kristin's tongue worked her clit. Both girls teetered on the brink of orgasm as Derrick slid his cock from Stephanie and thrust it into Kristin's mouth. Kristin sucked every drop of Stephanie from Derrick's cock, and she craved more of Stephanie's sweet pussy. He went back and forth between Stephanie's pussy and Kristin's mouth until he couldn't hold back any longer.

Kristin moaned in orgasm from Stephanie's tongue as Derrick's large cock rode against her lips. Kristin felt his cock throbbing in her mouth, and he pulled it out as it began to cum. Derrick stroked his cock with his hand as he was cumming all over Stephanie's ass. His creamy load ran down the crack of Stephanie's ass and dripped onto Kristin's adorable, sun-kissed face, and she didn't hesitate to lap up every drop she could get.

Without skipping a beat, Kristin lifted her head and went right back to finishing Stephanie. Her lips wrapped around Stephanie's clit and she sucked as her tongue swirled around. Kristin alternated between this and licking Stephanie's pussy in a variety of patterns until she felt Stephanie collapse on top of her while screaming.

Once Stephanie had finished, she turned and adjusted her position so she was now face to face with Kristin. Stephanie saw Kristin's face was covered in cum, and she used her finger to scoop each ounce into Kristin's thirsty mouth. Before Kristin could swallow, Stephanie began kissing her, and their two tongues danced in a mixture of Derrick's hot, salty cum. Stephanie collapsed next to Kristin, and the two girls held each other as Derrick walked off to the bathroom. They exchanged gentle kisses and lightly caressed the other's bodies.

"Will I ever see you again?" Kristin asked.

Stephanie softly replied, "Maybe."

"Only maybe? How can I turn that into a *definitely*?"

"You have my number; see if you can convince me." Stephanie continued, "But we really have to go. I have to be at work early tomorrow, and I can't be late. I already think my boss is starting to hate me."

"Thank you," Kristin sincerely said.

"For what?" Stephanie asked as she got off the bed and began putting her shirt on.

"For just being you. I had a great time tonight, and I needed it," answered Kristin.

"I needed it, too."

Derrick returned from the bathroom, and Stephanie ran in to quickly clean up and put herself back together before they left. Derrick drove Stephanie to her car, parked just around the corner from his apartment, and asked, "Are you sure you don't want to come up and change?"

She said, "No, I'm okay. I have my bag, and I'll just change really quick in the car. I really need to go, and I have a feeling I'll stay longer if I go upstairs with you."

"You know there's no way I'd let you leave!"

"Exactly, bad boy. Now shut up, and kiss me."

After saying their good nights, Stephanie grabbed her things from Derrick's car and got in her own. She watched him drive off, as she slid a pair of workout shorts under her skirt, and she then took off the skirt, stockings, and heels which she replaced with a pair of flip-flops. She contemplated leaving the button down top on, but she saw no one was around and quickly changed into a more comfortable tee shirt.

Stephanie started her long drive home, and she saw it was already twelve-thirty in the morning. She quickly did the math, calculating when she'd get home, how long she would take to get ready, and what time she needed to be up for work, and she realized she would only get little more than a few hours of sleep. Although she was dreading the following day, she thought to herself, *tonight was so worth it.*

Stephanie was traveling south on Route 24, nearing her exit, when she saw a car driving behind her, catching up to her at a very rapid pace. The headlights drew closer and closer, and the vehicle appeared to be accelerating even more when it changed lanes to get directly behind her. The vehicle was zealously tailgating her, and she uttered to herself, *what is this jerk doing?*

Suddenly, the vehicle's headlights began to alternate back and forth, and she was flooded with a burst of blue strobe lights. A few blasts of the siren, and Stephanie began to pull over in the breakdown lane while yelling, *Shit! Shit! Shit!*

A tall, well-built man in a crisply sharp uniform approached her driver's side window. Stephanie lowered the window, and she was greeted with, "Good evening ma'am. I'm Trooper Shea with the Massachusetts State Police. May I have your driver's license and registration, please?"

"Of course you can," Stephanie replied as she began fumbling through her purse for the items.

The trooper saw her schoolgirl outfit and heels on the front seat, and he said, "Ma'am, have you been drinking tonight?"

"No, not at all, sir."

"I ask because you're driving with your headlights off – you only have your parking lights on, you've passed your license three times without seeing it while you were looking for it in your wallet, and I'm getting the very distinct odor of alcohol when you speak. So, I'm going to ask you again, have you had anything to drink tonight?"

Stephanie insisted she had nothing to drink, and the trooper had her step out of her car. He requested her to perform a field sobriety test, and Stephanie responded,

"I'm a District Attorney, and I know my rights. I know you can't make me do your tests."

The trooper confidently replied, "If that's the case, then you also know that your refusal to do a field sobriety test will result in your immediate arrest. Are you sure that's the route you want to go?"

"Please, sir," Stephanie begged. "I had two drinks, that's all, just two drinks. If I get arrested I could lose everything. Please don't do this."

"Ma'am, if you've only had two drinks, you should have no problem with the test I'd like to perform, and then I'll be happy to send you off on your way. But right now, you only have two choices: do the test or go to jail."

"Look," Stephanie said. "I'll do anything if you look the other way, literally anything. We can go anywhere you want, and I'll do anything you want." The tears began streaming down her face as she realized what she was saying. She begged, "Please don't do this to me."

"Ma'am, I want to inform you that there is a dash camera in my police cruiser, and I'm equipped with a microphone. All of our actions are being recorded, and this can all be used as evidence in court. I'm only going to ask you one last time -- are you going to comply with my request to conduct a field sobriety test?"

Stephanie replied, "No."

She heard the ratcheting clicks of the cold, steel handcuffs securing her wrists behind her back as the trooper announced, "I'm placing you under arrest for suspicion of operating a motor vehicle while under the influence of alcohol." He continued, "You have the right to remain silent, anything you say can be used against you in a court of law. You have the right to have an attorney present during any and all questioning, and if you cannot afford an attorney, one will be provided for you. If you decide to answer any questions, you can stop at any time. Do you understand the rights I just read to you?"

"Yes," Stephanie said as the surreal feeling of the situation faded into the frightening reality of what was happening.

Oh my God, I'm being arrested. This is actually happening, she thought as she sat in the rear of the trooper's cruiser. She watched as the trooper searched her car, and he then walked back to the cruiser and opened the rear door to speak with her.

"Ma'am, do you know what this is?" he asked while holding out his hand.

Stephanie saw a single Vicodin pill in his palm. She knew it must have been one she got from Derrick, but she answered, "No, it's not mine."

"Well, I just found it in your purse." The trooper paused before continuing, "It will take me about twenty minutes to call poison control, wait on hold, give them the number stamped on the side, and have them tell me what this is, or you can just be honest and tell me right now. The end result is the same either way, but you can just save me a lot of time."

"I think I need a lawyer," Stephanie mumbled between tears.

"I think you're right," the trooper commented before closing the car door. "Is there anyone you'd like me to call for you?"

"My husband, Jacob," she reluctantly answered.

● ● ●

9

Walking Out

Jacob was woken from a sound sleep by the vibration of his cell phone on the nightstand. He hurried to find the phone in the darkness, and he answered with a concerned, "Hello?"

The man on the other end of the phone asked, "Is this Jacob Bradford?"

"It is, and who is this?"

The caller replied, "Sir, my name is Trooper Shea with the Massachusetts State Police."

Jacob suddenly recalled Stephanie was not home, and he quickly snapped to his senses and asked, "The State Police?" He sat up in bed as he continued, "Is everything okay?"

"Well, sir, I wouldn't exactly say everything is okay, but everyone is safe and sound. Unfortunately, your wife, Stephanie Bradford, is being arrested for driving a vehicle while intoxicated as well as a narcotics possession charge."

Jacob asked, "Are you sure you have the right Stephanie Bradford?"

"I'm afraid I do, Mr. Bradford - she provided me with your number. The reason I'm calling is regarding the white Volvo she was operating this evening. It's registered in your name, and I was wondering if you'd like to arrange for a private tow rather than have me impound the vehicle."

"Un-fucking-believable," Jacob said in disbelief. "Alright, yeah I'd much rather have the car towed to the house."

"I just can't arrange that for you," the trooper explained. "But if you can find a company that will respond in the next few minutes, I'll be more than happy to stand by with your vehicle."

"Thank you, so much. Where exactly are you?"

"We're on the southbound side of Route 24, just south of 106 in Bridgewater. The tow driver will see my lights."

Jacob thanked the trooper again, and he began calling tow truck companies until he found one willing to get his car from the highway. Jacob returned the phone call to Trooper Shea, "Hi Trooper, there is a tow truck from Reynolds' Towing on their way to get the car now."

"Good deal! Did they give you an estimated arrival time?"

"They said they'll be with you in twenty minutes."

"That works," said Trooper Shea. "Would you like to talk to your wife before we hang up?"

"No," replied Jacob. "I have nothing left to say to her."

Just less than an hour later, Jacob heard the loud beeping of the tow truck backing into his driveway with Stephanie's Volvo attached to the back. Jacob walked to the front yard where he waited in the grass for the car to be released.

"That'll be two hundred cash," said the driver.

"Damn, you guys really know when you have someone by the balls," Jacob said as he counted out the money and handed it to the driver.

The driver folded the stack of tens and twenties, and he placed the money in his shirt pocket. He started lowering the car and said, "Hey, it beats the shit out of having the car impounded. You'd pay for the tow, the storage fee, and all that other crap. It would end up costing you twice as much."

"You sure know how to sugar coat something, don't you?"

"Bet your ass I do," the burly driver said with a laugh. "Before I go, we just have to go over the property in the car. I did an inventory sheet with the trooper, and he signed it to verify what was in the car when I left the scene. Now, I just need you to look over the property and give your signature saying it's all still there."

Jacob began to look through Stephanie's car, and he saw the schoolgirl skirt, her stockings, and her heels. He then went to the trunk where he found the crumpled up parking ticket and a man's belt that didn't belong to him. Jacob stopped looking through the car, and he signed the form. As the tow truck driver left, Jacob walked into the house carrying the brown belt he found in the trunk.

Jacob was torn over his decision, and while he already knew he was making the right decision, he now knew with certainty that leaving Stephanie was the best thing he could do. He walked to the bedroom and sat at the edge of the bed, holding his cell phone in his hand, waiting for the call from Stephanie, which he was certain would come, needing him to bail her out of jail. He thought to himself, *I know that shithead she's sleeping with isn't going to get her out, so of course she'll call me.*

Jacob was angry and even disgusted by Stephanie and what she had done, but for some unexplained reason he still wanted to help her. Whether it was a sign of the love he had for her, or his own selfish desire to be there for her just one last time, he sat patiently waiting for Stephanie's call.

• • •

The sun was just beginning to dawn on a new morning as Stephanie was being released from jail on her own recognizance. She was escorted from her cell and walked down a long hallway. The generic quality tile floor, white cinder block walls, and bright fluorescent lights gave the jail facility a cold feeling that felt lost and abandoned.

Stephanie was wearing a jail-issued yellow jumpsuit, white socks, and cheap flip-flops. As she arrived at the Release and Property Return Window, she was given a large plastic bag with her clothes and other belongings.

"You need to change into your own clothes, and leave the facility's clothes in the laundry bin on your left. You can keep the shower shoes," instructed a very butch female deputy.

Stephanie looked around inquisitively and asked, "Where can I change?"

"This isn't Nordstrom's, darling, and we don't have fitting rooms. You can change right here."

"Right here?"

The deputy responded, "Ma'am, we're trying to release you, but if you want to give us a hard time, we can turn you around and take you right back to a cell."

"No, I'm sorry. You're right," said Stephanie as she began disrobing in front of the deputy.

Her property, including her purse and cell phone, were returned to her and she was escorted to the jail's exit. As she walked through the last secured point, the large metal door closed behind her and slammed with a loud bang. Stephanie stood at the main entrance to the jail facility with no idea what she was going to do next.

Stephanie powered her cell phone on, and her eyes began to tear as she waited for the phone to finish rebooting. As it did, and she saw she had a signal, she contemplated whether she would call Jacob or Derrick. Stephanie knew there was only one person she could turn to for help in absolutely any situation, and she started the call.

Jacob was still sitting in bed, waiting for the phone call from Stephanie, when his phone alerted to an incoming call. "Hello," he answered on the first ring.

"Baby, it's me," Stephanie said while crying. "I need you to help me. I don't even know where to begin…"

"I already talked to Trooper Shea, and he told me what happened. What do you need from me?"

"I don't know where my car is, I don't know how I'm going to get home, and I have no idea what I'm going to do," cried Stephanie.

"Your car is here at the house. Just tell me where you are, and I'll come get you."

Stephanie gratefully stated, "My God, Jacob, thank you. I'm at the Plymouth County Jail. And Jacob, please don't tell anybody...please!"

"I don't know why you wouldn't want me to say anything, something like this won't stay a secret for very long. Either way, I'll be there in a little while," said Jacob before hanging up the phone.

Jacob thought in silence as he drove to pick up Stephanie, and arrived to find her sitting on the curb in front of the jail. Even at her worst, she looked adorable in her little shorts and tight T-shirt. She got in the car with neither of them saying a single word to the other. Stephanie spent nearly the entire ride home in complete silence out of fear and humiliation, and Jacob remained lost for words from sheer anger.

Stephanie looked out of the passenger side window as Jacob drove, and she entered deep thought. Everything suddenly came into focus, and for the first time in a long time, she saw things very clearly. It was like someone had twisted a kaleidoscope, and what was once a distorted confusing image was now clear and beautiful.

When she needed someone the most, it was Jacob who was there for her without question. Jacob was obviously angry with her, and Stephanie knew their relationship was in trouble, but he was still willing to drop everything to come save her. Stephanie saw, more than ever, that Jacob was the rock in her life. He may not have been the most adventurous, outgoing, or exciting man, but he was stable and safe. He never lured her into doing anything that would be detrimental to her future, and he was always there to build her up or catch her when she fell. Jacob was her shelter from any storm.

Having no idea Jacob already knew about Derrick, she looked over at him and thought, *I can't believe I almost threw this marriage away. I can't believe I almost lost Jacob.*

As the drive was nearing its end and they were just minutes from their house, Stephanie finally spoke and asked, "Did you look in my car, Jacob?"

"I did," he replied without any sign of emotion.

Stephanie became extremely nervous because of the clothing she left in her car when she was arrested. "Did you see the outfit I put together to wear for you?" she asked very unconvincingly.

"For me?" Jacob replied. "If it's for me, why does it look like it had been worn very recently?"

"I had to try it on, silly, to see if it still fits," said Stephanie with a crack in her voice.

Before Jacob could retort, he turned into their driveway, and Stephanie saw the moving truck Jacob rented. "Why is that there?" she asked.

Jacob stared straight ahead without removing his hands from the steering wheel or looking at Stephanie. He dug deep for the courage to blurt out what needed to be said, and he replied, "I'm leaving you. I'm moving out, today."

"Leaving me? What? I know we've had our problems lately, but it's no reason to ruin our marriage." She reached her hand to Jacob, placed it on his forearm, and continued, "We can fix this -- we can work through it."

"Work through what?" Jacob asked. "Let's just pretend for a minute that I believe you about the skirt and shoes in your car being for me, how can you explain some other man's belt in your trunk?"

Stephanie worked up a fake laugh, and answered, "That's what this is about? That's not another man's belt, it's your belt. I brought a bunch of your old clothes to the Goodwill box, and it must have fallen out of the bag. You honestly don't remember wearing that belt when we first met?"

Still cold as an arctic chill, Jacob asked, "Then the parking ticket in your trunk – who were you going to see near Boston Common?"

Stephanie struggled for a reply and began, "That was from when – it was the night that..." until she was abruptly stopped by Jacob.

"Stephanie, stop the bullshit. You want to know what this is about?" Jacob retrieved the small digital voice recorder from the car's center console and pressed play as he said, "This is what it's about..."

As the recorder played, Stephanie instantly recognized Derrick's voice:

I just have two stringing along right now. One is a little blonde that I've been tapping for a while, and she's starting to get a little on the boring side - kind of reached my end with her. But my most recent one, is a tight little brunette that's a shit ton of fun.

Stephanie had the intense feeling of fear that we have all experienced at least once in our lives. The feeling when we were just caught doing something that we know is about to get us in deep, life-altering trouble. She felt the frightening sensation of being caught with nowhere to run, and she had absolutely no idea of what to do next. She had no excuse or explanation, but despite all of that, she wasn't yet willing to concede to telling the truth.

"Jacob, it's not what you think, I was only..."

"Stop!" Jacob shouted. "After everything you've done, everything you've been doing, the very least you could do is show me enough dignity to be honest with me."

"Okay, I will. I'll be honest and tell you the truth about anything you ask me. What do you want to know?"

He replied, "I already know more than I ever thought I wanted to. All that is left is to hear it directly from you - have you been sleeping with another man?"

She looked down towards the floor of the car, tears streaming down her face, and struggling to breathe, and she barely answered, "Please don't leave me."

"Answer me!" Jacob demanded. "I want to hear you say it."

"Yes," she answered. "I slept with another man. Just please don't leave me."

"I already left, Stephanie," said Jacob. "I'm moving everything I want out of the house, today. I don't really care where you go, but I don't want you here while I'm doing it. I already opened a new bank account, and I took half of our savings. I want to sell the house and split whatever is left after the sale. After that, we go our separate ways. I think I'm being extremely fair."

Stephanie sniffled, "You are, Jacob. I don't even deserve that."

Jacob coldly snapped, "You're right, you don't," before telling Stephanie to get ready for work so he can finish moving.

Jacob told Stephanie that he would be keeping the Volvo and she could have his car. He then said he wanted to go for a drive, and he asked her to not be there when he returned. Jacob didn't want Stephanie to be there while he finished moving due to his trepidation that she may convince him to stay. Stephanie reluctantly agreed, but only because she knew she had no room for argument. She knew her marriage was beyond salvageable, and she walked away from the car as Jacob drove off.

Stephanie looked at Jacob's soft, gentle face as she got out of what was once her car. His face showed the pain which she had caused him, and it broke her heart to know she had so badly hurt the man who loved her so much. As she looked at Jacob's face, she knew beyond any shadow of a doubt, she just lost the very best thing that would ever happen to her.

Stephanie took a shower and did her best to get ready for her day, but the sound of Derrick's voice on the recorder saying, *I just have two stringing along right now. One is a little blonde that I've been tapping for a while*, resonated over and over within her head. At that moment, Stephanie was not only dealing with the loss of Jacob, she was also facing the reality that Derrick was not the man she had thought he was.

She stood before the mirror as she got dressed, and she stopped to just look at herself. Making decisions is easy; it's living with the consequences of our decisions that is hard. This lesson was like a punch to Stephanie's gut as she had to look at herself in the mirror and try to accept what she had done.

She slid on a pair of cute jeans, a pink hoodie, and a pair of Converse low-top chucks, and Stephanie left the house to face her day.

Stephanie called Bill Webber, and much to her relief, his line went to voicemail. "Hi, Bill. It's me Stephanie," she started. "I'm not feeling well at all today, so I'm going to stay home and try to get some rest. I'll be in tomorrow, and I hope you're not mad."

Stephanie never liked driving Jacob's Jeep, but now, she didn't have a choice.

• • •

Stephanie drove aimlessly for a short time before she convinced herself to indulge in a bit of retail therapy. Jacob was moving out, and she now had the house all to herself. This meant there was no longer the need to compromise on decorating, and she could do whatever she wanted.

For as long as she could remember, Stephanie was the "half glass full" kind of girl who always tried to make the best out of any situation. This quality likely rose from her being raised in a broken home by a highly irresponsible mother. She often considered herself to be raised more by her grandmother than her actual mother, but the fact of the matter is, Stephanie primarily raised herself from a very young age. Her neglected childhood taught her several lessons: she learned quite early on that she and only she was responsible for her actions, she learned that only hard work and perseverance would lead to her success, and most importantly, she learned to always try to find something positive in even the worst situations.

Stephanie aimed her car for the nearest Ikea, and she pressed her foot on the accelerator. Before long, she walked through the entrance and selected a large cart. She opened her purse and removed a credit card from her wallet. Stephanie was never the most responsible person with credit, and Jacob allowed her to have only one card to be used for emergencies only. *Jacob's gone now,* she thought, *and I can use this card for anything I want.*

Four hours later, Stephanie returned home with a Jeep full of home decorations and a freshly maxed out credit card.

Stephanie walked into the house to find Jacob was already gone. She walked into her now half-empty home, and the bareness of the rooms reminded her of when she and Jacob first moved in. She reminisced of her and her husband running through the home, playing together like children, and being so excited to start a life together. This was supposed to be the home where they would have started a family, made memories, and grown old together. Now, however, it was just an empty house filled with shattered dreams.

Stephanie saw that Jacob had cleaned out the Volvo before leaving with it, and the contents from the car were thrown across the living room floor. Stephanie crouched down to the items, and she could only imagine Jacob's pain as she looked at the plaid skirt, heels, and perhaps worst of all, Derrick's belt. She picked them, rolling everything in a single ball, and dropped them in the corner of the room.

She spent the rest of the day re-organizing her home and hanging the new pictures, knick-knacks, and other wall art she purchased. She basically tried to fill her day with anything that would help keep her mind off of everything she had going on in her life. For just one day, Stephanie wanted to be free.

As the day turned into night, Stephanie was winding down and preparing to get ready for bed. From the master bathroom, she looked to her bedroom as she brushed her teeth, and she saw her empty bed. To look at the bed, and not see Jacob reading while he waited for her to join him, completely negated any value her retail therapy may have added to her day.

Stephanie heard her phone chime to the tone of an incoming text message. She trotted to her phone and found the message to be from Derrick.

"Able to sneak out tonight, bad girl?" he asked.

What an asshole, Stephanie thought as she powered down her phone without responding. She was surprised by how little hurt she was feeling for her inevitable loss of someone who she thought meant so much to her. After hearing the recording of Derrick over and over in her head, Stephanie knew she was finished with him. The only uncertainty she had was whether to sit down and discuss it with him like an adult, or just let him figure it out by changing her number and completely avoiding him.

Regardless of what was to come, Stephanie was forced to deal with her life in the moment she was currently in. She pulled back the covers and crawled into bed. Even though she was all alone, she still stayed on her side of the mattress, curled up in the blankets as she drifted off to sleep.

• • •

10

A Friend in Need

Stephanie shot up to a seated position and instantly woke up, from the deepest sleep, to a brightly lit room. She looked to see what time it was, and as she saw the alarm clock was missing from Jacob's nightstand she thought, *Really Jacob? Even the alarm clock?*

She began a mad dash to get ready for work as her phone powered on. With her hair quickly pulled back in a ponytail, she slid into a pair of gray dress slacks, a light blue, short sleeved button down, and a pair of comfortable black flats. After getting ready in just eleven minutes, she was out the door in record time.

Stephanie arrived to work, and although she was more than an hour late, given the events of the past couple of days, she was grateful to have even made it at all. After everything that had happened, the last thing she wanted to do was face Bill Webber, but her thought process was so irrational and disorganized, she was more concerned about being late to work than dealing with her arrest.

People looked at her strangely as she ran through the lobby of her building trying to make it to her office as quickly as possible. She boarded the elevator and pressed the button for her floor, but the elevator car felt like someone had purposely slowed it down just to screw with her. Of course, the elevator was filled with riders getting off on nearly every floor, and the ascent was slowed even more. When the doors finally slid open on her floor, Stephanie was terrified to go to her office.

She walked briskly past Webber's office on the way to her own, and she was relieved to see he wasn't there. *Maybe he's not in yet*, she thought, but unfortunately this hope was dashed when she saw Webber standing in her office as she approached.

She saw two interns with him, and together they were packing her files from the Hutchinson case into a cardboard box. She rudely asked, "What do you guys think you're doing?" as she entered the small room.

Webber exploded, "Who the hell do you think you are asking me a question like that?" He directed the interns out of the office, and as he closed the door behind them, he continued, "Bradford, I put my reputation on the line for you. I put my God damned name on the line to put you as lead on this case, and every step of the way, you've gone and done whatever you could to screw it up. A few months ago, I thought you were the future of this office, but now, I don't know what the hell your future even is."

"You already know what happened the other night, don't you?" Stephanie timidly asked.

"One of my attorneys gets arrested for DUI and possession of hydrocodone and then identifies herself as a District Attorney to the arresting Trooper -- yes, Bradford, I tend to hear about this kind of thing very quickly."

"Mr. Webber, I know this looks bad, and I know I can't be directly on the case anymore, but please don't pull me off completely. This case means so much to me; please, let me see it through."

Webber looked at Stephanie with a look of complete disbelief on his face. "Are you serious? Do you truly believe I would let you anywhere near this case? Do you think I would let you prosecute a DUI homicide, after you got a DUI yourself?" Webber paused before continuing, "Is that what you think this is about, pulling you from the case? Do you think that's what I'm doing?"

"Yes, well that's what I thought. Do you mean you're not pulling me off?"

"Bradford, it's always something, and it's just getting to be too much. You're either leaving work without telling anyone, calling in sick, not showing up for court, and now this. Stephanie, I'm not pulling you off the case. I don't know how to say this, but…" Webber paused before finishing, "Bradford, I'm terminating you. I'm sorry, but your fired."

"No, Bill, please don't fire me," she pleaded. "I'm begging you, please. I can't lose this job, it means everything to me."

"Bradford, I'm sorry, but there's just nothing more I can do for you. It's over. I'll give you ten minutes to gather your personal items from your desk and say goodbye. If you don't leave after that, I'm going to have you escorted out by security."

"Bill, please don't do this to me! You don't understand, you can't do this to me!"

"Don't you dare put this on me," Webber scorned. "I'm not doing anything *to* you. You damn well did this to yourself. Now get your things and go."

Stephanie watched with sorrow as Webber walked away. He was once her mentor, and he looked at her as his protégé of sorts, but now he couldn't even look at her. She grabbed her purse and ran to Karen's office. At that moment, she needed Karen more than anything, but she found Karen's office empty. "Where's Karen?" Stephanie yelled to Karen's assistant.

"She called in sick, Stephanie. Are you alright?" answered Karen's assistant from her desk right outside Karen's office.

"No! No! No!" Stephanie cried as she ran towards the elevators with nearly the entire office watching in horror as the events were unfolding before them.

Stephanie tried to call Karen multiple times as she rode the elevator toward the lobby, but each call went to voicemail. "Where are you, Karen? I need you, please call me back," she said in the voicemail as she reached the lobby and exited to the street.

Stephanie stood on the bustling city sidewalk in the heart of downtown Boston, and she looked around, almost in a daze, as her world was inexplicably crashing down all around her. She needed someone to turn to – she needed anyone who could be there for her, but for the first time in her life, she felt as though she had no one. In her moment of immense suffering and vulnerability, she decided to reach for the only person she could, and she opted to disregard the recording of Derrick which she had heard.

I don't care what was on that recording, I know Derrick loves me, Stephanie irrationally thought as she placed a call to his phone. The call went straight to voicemail without ringing, and she knew he had turned his phone off. *Why, Derrick, why today?*

Stephanie assumed Derrick was at work, and she drove to the coffee shop to wait for him. She quickly snatched up the only empty seat by the window where she had a clear view to the front of Derrick's building. As the day drew on, she impatiently waited and waited. Each time the doorman would open the door, she would only be disappointed to see someone other than Derrick walking from within. That was until the door opened, and Stephanie saw not Derrick, but another familiar face leave the building.

Dressed in a seductively short denim skirt, tall heels, and a snug-fitting, dark blue tee, Karen walked from

Derrick's apartment building, and she quickly rounded the corner and strutted out of Stephanie's sight.

Stephanie wanted to run to confront Karen, but her body was paralyzed with shock. She felt numb, and it took more than a minute before she could move, much less think of what she would possibly say to Karen. When she snapped out of her fog of shock and back to reality, Stephanie marched straight to the front door of Derrick's building.

The doorman had become used to seeing Stephanie, and he greeted her with a smile; however, he kindly reminded her he was not able to allow her into the building.

"Look," said Stephanie with anger. "I just saw my friend, my best friend, walk out of here, and you know exactly what the fuck is going on. You do whatever you have to do, but I'm going in there and confronting him right now."

"I feel for you, believe me, I do. However, it doesn't change the fact that I'm not authorized to let anyone in without a resident being present," he reminded Stephanie for a second time.

"Imagine if it were you standing here, having your life shattered. Even worse, imagine it was your daughter or your sister standing here instead of me. What would you do if it was someone you loved?"

The doorman stood silent for a short moment before gently nodding his head and stepping to the side while opening the door.

Bam! Bam! Bam! Stephanie slammed on the door of Derrick's apartment. The knock echoed down the long industrial-style hallway, and she had no idea what she would even say to Derrick when he answered. She kept banging.

Derrick opened the door, shirtless and wearing only a pair of workout pants, and he said, "Oh fuck... What are you doing here?"

Stephanie asked, "What the fuck am I doing here? Seriously? That's what you have to say to me right now?"

"How did you get up here?"

"The doorman let me up."

"He's fired," Derrick calmly replied. "You're obviously pissed, and I'm not stupid. I know you must have seen her, so now you know."

"Now I know what Derrick? I don't know anything, other than the fact that I just saw my best friend walk out of here. How the hell did Karen even meet you?"

"Look, it's just whatever now." Derrick coldly said. He held the door barely open and positioned himself in a manner which indicated Stephanie was not invited in. He folded his arms and continued, "What do you want from me?"

"Derrick, what the hell is going on? I thought you were falling in love with me?"

"I don't know what to say. You caught me, and it's over. If you want to forget about what you saw, I'm cool with that. But if not, then it just is what it is."

"It is what it is? I thought you loved me. I lost everything for you!"

As Stephanie was losing Jacob, and then losing her job, she thought her life couldn't get any lower. She thought she had hit rock bottom. Now that she was standing at Derrick's door, listening to what he had to say, she knew she had thrown it all away for nothing. The realization that it was all a lie was the proverbial salt in Stephanie's wound which made her emotional pain agonizing.

She broke down and begged Derrick, "Please, tell me why. Why did you do this to me?"

Derrick, completely unfazed by Stephanie's intense emotion, cruelly said, "You were for fun. I'm sorry, but it was nothing more. If you got the wrong idea and thought there was something more between us, that's your problem and not mine."

Stephanie started to remind Derrick of the things he had said to her, and the emotions he shared, but Derrick just closed the door without offering even the slightest hint of an explanation. Everything Derrick said was a lie. She heard him lock the deadbolt on the other side of the door, and she fell to the ground crying.

While lying on the cold, hard concrete floor, Stephanie cried and screamed, "I fucking hate you, Derrick! I fucking hate you!"

• • •

Stephanie walked to her car, and before long, her phone began ringing. She looked at the display and saw the incoming call was from Karen. She knew Karen was either calling because she had just heard Stephanie had been fired or because Karen just heard from Derrick. Regardless of the reason for the call, Stephanie had no desire to even speak with Karen, and she ignored the call. Karen called repeatedly, but Stephanie knew there was nothing Karen could say that could even begin to fix Stephanie's situation, and she ignored each subsequent call just as she had done the first.

As Stephanie sat in the car, trying to calm herself enough to safely drive, her phone alerted to an incoming text from Karen which read, **"Steph, please answer. Derrick told me what happened, but you need to let me explain. It's not what you think."**

Stephanie replied, **"It's exactly what I think. Stop calling me."**

"No, Stephanie, it's not what you think. You need to let me explain this to you. You need to know what is happening."

"My life is over, Karen," typed Stephanie. **"In one day, my whole entire world just disappeared...that's what is happening."**

Stephanie's phone began ringing with another call from Karen. Stephanie ignored this call as well, and Karen followed with the text message, **"Stephanie, please answer."**

"Stop calling me!" messaged Stephanie.

Suddenly, Stephanie's phone began receiving a stream of incoming text messages from Karen, and she gathered it was actually one very long text message arriving in pieces. She began reading the extensive message as it arrived,

"Stephanie, you need to know this. Derrick isn't who you think he is. I've known him for more than two years, and it's not a coincidence that he met you. I met him and I had a very short affair with him, but I broke it off after I started seeing the real him. He became so angry over me breaking up with him, and he refused to let me go. While I was with him, he took pictures of me doing things, sometimes very humiliating things, and he held those pictures over me. I basically became his fucking sex slave with him threatening to send the pictures to my husband, my family, my neighbors, and my co-workers if I didn't do every last thing he said. Then he used those pictures to make me take even more pictures and videos, and it formed a cycle where I feel like he owns me. He does own me, and he knows it."

"What does any of this have to do with me?" asked Stephanie.

Karen's response began arriving on Stephanie's phone, "One day, about a week before you met him, he was picking me up from work. He saw me walking out with you, and he told me he wanted to have sex with you. He forced me to make it happen." Karen continued to explain, "The day you met him, I told him where you were going to be, and that's why I didn't go to lunch with you."

"You knew what he was doing to you, and you just unleashed him on me?"

"I tried to stop it, I really did. After you first met him, I told you it was a bad idea. I figured if I did my part, by setting him up with you, and you just weren't interested, he'd leave it alone, but he didn't. After you broke up with him, he told me he would ruin me if I didn't convince you to go back to him."

Stephanie fell into shock as she read each word of Karen's explanation. While she was having a hard time wrapping her head around the whole thing, one aspect was utterly confusing to Stephanie, and she asked, "If he only wanted to have sex with me, why didn't he just let it go after he did?"

"Because he's sick, Stephanie. He was going to be done and break it off with you after he got what he wanted, but you broke it off with him first. You beat him to it, and he was furious that you broke up with him. He told me he was going to make you pay for doing that."

"Make me pay? For breaking up with him? Pay how?" asked Stephanie.

"By ruining your life," said Karen. "I told you, he's sick. He wanted you to leave Jacob for him, and the minute you did, he was going to drop you. He just wanted to ruin your life."

"You knew all this, and you let him do it? You were supposed to be my fucking friend, you cunt." replied Stephanie, with her head swirling in the disbelief that her best friend had led her into such an atrocious trap. "You destroyed my life, Karen. Not Derrick, you!"

"I'm so sorry, Stephanie, but you don't understand. I'm afraid of him. I'm so afraid of him. He owns me, he uses me, and I know he's going to just throw me away when he's done. You have no idea what he does, what kind of things he makes me do."

"So, you set me up to fall into the same shit? God damn, Karen!" Stephanie said.

"Please, Stephanie, please let me say I'm sorry to your face. After that, if you never want to look at me again, I'll completely understand. I'll give anything to say I'm sorry to you."

Stephanie wanted to hate Karen with every ounce of her being, but she just couldn't. As angry, betrayed, and hurt as she was by Karen, she just couldn't bring herself to hate her. Stephanie replied, "I'm tired, I'm confused,

I'm scared, and I'm hurt. I'm going home, so you can meet me there if you want."

"I just need to go home and change clothes, and I'll meet you there," replied Karen.

Stephanie drove home in a cloud of complete shock. She not only contemplated what she would say to Karen when she saw her, but also what she was going to do with her now shredded life. Her world was a house of cards which had just collapsed, and she lost her husband, her boyfriend, her best friend, her job, and she even faced the prospect of going to jail. The one person in the world who Stephanie could always turn to for help with anything was gone, and she had no idea how to face this on her own. She was falling deeper and deeper into the abyss.

• • •

Expecting Karen to arrive at any moment, Stephanie began cleaning up some of the clutter laying around her house. She picked up the ball of clothing which had come from her car, and she placed all but the brown leather belt in a nearby laundry basket. Stephanie stared at the belt, remembering the first time she saw Derrick wearing it, and although she had regained her composure, she was still unable to fathom the depth of the lies in which she had become entangled. She was instantly pulled from her deep thought by the sound of a knock on her front door.

She held the belt in her hand as she answered the door. She opened the door to find Karen outside, and she invited her in. Stephanie handed the belt to Karen, and greeted her with, "Here, give this to Derrick next time you see him."

Karen and Stephanie began talking, and the two women just rehashed the same issues which they had already battled through in their earlier conversation of text messages. It was obvious to Stephanie that Karen was coming apart at the seams, and she saw how devastated Karen was. Stephanie tried her best to console Karen, but it was just too difficult for her to be fake.

Stephanie said, "Karen, I understand where you're coming from, or at least I'm trying to understand. I get that you're scared, and for that part, I guess I understand. But I want *you* to understand something, too -- I will never forgive you for this. No matter what you say or what you do, I will never accept you as my friend again, and I will never forgive you."

Karen showed Stephanie a string of text messages she had been receiving from Derrick since Stephanie confronted him. In the messages, Derrick was blaming Karen for Stephanie catching them, and he called Karen the most horrific names. The most terrifying messages, though, were the multiple texts threatening to ruin her life. The final message from Derrick to Karen read,

"I'm going to destroy you, you stupid bitch. You and your little fucking friend," and it mortified both of them.

Stephanie convinced Karen that it was time to end Derrick's grip over her life. Karen decided she would call his bluff, let Derrick do as he wanted with the photos of her, and she would ultimately deal with the aftermath as it came. She wasn't going to be his slave any longer.

The two women talked well into the night, with Karen realizing that very much like Stephanie's, her life as she knew it was about to end.

Stephanie ended the conversation by announcing, "I'm exhausted, Karen. I need to go take a shower and go bed."

"Can I stay just a little longer?" asked Karen. "I can't let my husband find out about this from Derrick -- I need to tell him everything when I get home tonight, myself. I need to come completely clean, and I'm just not ready to go yet."

"Stay as long as you want. Just lock the door when you leave," said Stephanie as she started to walk up the stairs to the master bathroom.

"Stephanie," Karen called out.

Stephanie stopped, and without looking at Karen she replied, "Yes?"

"Please tell me you might forgive me someday. I'm about to lose everything, and I can't lose you, too."

"I already told you, Karen. I'll never forgive you for this, never. Oh, and welcome to my world," said Stephanie before she continued up the stairs.

Karen sat alone on the living room floor, and she started to imagine what was about to become of her life. Her mind raced with fear. She knew her co-workers and her husband would soon learn of her affair with Derrick, and she was certain Derrick would be sending them photos of her engaging in the most humiliating and degrading sex acts. She, too, would likely be losing her marriage and her career to Derrick, and facing that prospect was too much for her to handle.

The most painful prospect for Karen, however, was the thought of looking her loving husband in the eye and telling him her dark secret. Describing the things she had done with Derrick would devastate her husband, and Karen began to lose her grip on any rational thought as she realized she just couldn't do it.

Karen tightly gripped Derrick's belt in her right hand with enough force to turn her knuckles white, and she climbed the stairs to Stephanie's bedroom. She heard the shower running in the adjacent bathroom as she walked through the room, and she walked into Stephanie's closet. She used both hands to push Stephanie's hanging clothes to the side, revealing the garment rod at the top of the closet

Karen reached up and looped the belt through the garment rod and buckled the ends of the belt together. She stood on a storage bin and placed her head through the belt, forming a noose around her neck. She collapsed her knees, dropping her weight downward, and she hung herself in the closet. Stephanie was washing herself in the steam drenched shower, less than twenty feet away, as the spark of life quickly faded from Karen's body.

Ten minutes later, Stephanie walked into the bedroom from her shower, and she was drying her hair with a towel when she suddenly saw Karen's lifeless body hanging in her closet.

"No, Karen, no! Shit! Shit! Don't do this, Karen," shouted Stephanie as she worked to pull Karen free from the belt.

Karen, in her gray sweatpants and pink T-shirt, fell to the ground, and Stephanie rolled her to her back. She raced for her phone to call nine-one-one, but as she dialed nine-one, without pressing one a second time, she looked at Karen and knew she was gone. Stephanie looked at her phone, with her finger hovering over the digit to complete the call, but instead, she hung up the phone. Stephanie dropped to her knees, cradled Karen in her arms, and held her as she cried hysterically.

Stephanie continued to hold Karen as she thought back to the relationship the two once shared. The deep friendship she shared with Karen was something she thoroughly enjoyed, and Stephanie refused to allow Derrick to also steal the fond memories she had of Karen. She thought of the talks she had with Karen over lunch, she remembered the secrets they shared, and she remembered Karen always making her day a little brighter.

She saw the overly apparent death in Karen's face, and she gently stroked her soft blonde hair while saying, "I forgive you, Karen. Where ever you are right now, I forgive you with all my heart. You're still my best friend." She continued, "I hope God forgives me for what I'm about to do, but I'm going to make this bastard suffer for what he did. With everything I have, I'm going to make him suffer."

Stephanie's hatred for Derrick grew greater and greater the longer she held Karen's body. A boiling thirst for revenge grew inside of her until her until it manifested itself into a calculated plot within Stephanie's head.

She picked up the phone to call Jacob, and much to her surprise, he actually answered. Through her tears, she explained, "You need to listen to me, Jacob. I know you're leaving, and I do hate that, but I have to accept it. That's not why I'm calling, though."

"So why are you calling, Stephanie?"

She said, "I can't explain over the phone, but I know a lot more now than I did this morning. I need to tell you what I know, and I also need to make this son of a bitch pay for what he's done. I just need your help to do it -- I can't do it without you, Jacob. If there's any part of you that has ever loved me, please help me with this."

Stephanie waited for a response from Jacob, and she asked, "Will you help me?"

"Stephanie, don't start this. All I'm asking is for you to let me go, and please don't start playing games."

"Jacob, I'm not playing games. I need your help."

"I'm sure you do, Stephanie."

Stephanie pleaded with Jacob, "I know you're gone, and I know you're not coming back, but I just want to ask you this: how do you feel about the man I cheated with?"

"Give me a fucking break! You're seriously going to call me and start doing this?" Jacob asked as he started to become angry with Stephanie.

"God damn it, Jacob, answer me. For once in your fucking life, just one time, show some emotion about something. Show me that you're a human being for Christ's sake."

"Okay, you want to know how I feel about him?" yelled Jacob. "I want to cut his heart out of his chest, and I want to watch him die. But I can't do that, so you know what? I deal with it; I just deal with it, Stephanie."

"Jacob, I have a better idea, but you just have to trust me. There is a way for us to hurt him, and we can ruin his life the same way he ruined ours," Stephanie calmly explained. "You just have to trust me."

"What's your motivation for all of this? What did he do to *ruin* your life?"

"Jacob, I'm begging you. I need you more than anyone has ever needed another person before. Please come to the house and hear me out. If you want to get up and leave, I'll never bother you again, and I'll walk away for good. Please."

Jacob heard an intense pain in Stephanie's voice, and he ignored every sensible thought in his brain when he made the decision to go back to the house. Almost immediately upon his arrival, he learned of Karen's death, and he shifted his attention to consoling Stephanie.

He took Stephanie out of the house to get her away from what had happened, and they drove to the empty parking lot of a nearby shopping center. The two talked for hours, first about Karen and what had happened until Stephanie told Jacob the truth behind Derrick. Eventually the conversation shifted to Stephanie's plan for vengeance, and she walked Jacob through her idea.

Together, they fine-tuned the details of Stephanie's plan until Jacob said, "Do you really think this could work?"

"I know it could," Stephanie said with extreme confidence. "And I know it will."

Jacob replied, "Let's do it then. Start tomorrow?"

"We'll start tomorrow!"

• • •

11

Revenge is a Dish

Jacob drove Stephanie back to the house, and as he stopped the car in the driveway, he asked, "Are you sure you're ready to do this?"

"I am," said Stephanie. "But I just can't go back inside there."

"You don't have to. I'll do my part and take care of everything inside the house. Where are you going to stay?"

"I have no idea," Stephanie replied.

"It's okay. Just use your emergency credit card and stay in a hotel for a few nights. This should all be over by then."

Stephanie, scared to tell Jacob, said, "I used the emergency credit card to buy some things for the house."

"A hotel won't cost that much if you stay somewhere cheap. You left enough room on your card for that, right?"

"No, I maxed it out," Stephanie said with a look of embarrassment on her face.

"Are you shitting me, Stephanie?"

"Not now, Jacob. This seriously isn't the time."

Jacob reached his hand into his pocket to retrieve his wallet. He thumbed through the various cards inside until he pulled out a credit card with both his and Stephanie's name embossed on the front. He handed her the card and said, "Here, but please only use this for the hotel and nothing else. Promise?"

"I promise," she softly answered.

"Will you come in with me while I pack a bag?"

"But then you have to hurry. It's going to be daylight soon, and I have to hurry my ass up to make this work in time."

Stephanie and Jacob walked into the house, and Stephanie could still feel Karen in the air. She was glad Jacob was there since she knew she could never have gone back in alone. As she started to climb the stairs with Jacob, she suddenly stopped and said with panic, "I can't, Jacob. I can't go back in there. Please, don't make me go in there," as she started crying.

Jacob wrapped his arms around her, consoling her as he whispered, "Shhhh... It's okay, it's okay. You don't have to go in the bedroom. I'll go in and get whatever you need."

"No, I don't even want anything from inside there," she said as she started to calm down. "I don't want to wear anything that's in my closet. I just can't."

"That's fine," he said while continuing to hold her. "Use the credit card to buy some clothes in the morning, and also get whatever else you need to get you through the next few days. Is that better?"

"Yes," Stephanie said as she wiped the tears from beneath her eyes. She looked up at Jacob, as he was standing just inches from her, and she continued, "I'm so sorry Jacob. I really am."

"You promised me you wouldn't do this, Steph. I didn't come here for that."

"You're right, I'm just going to leave. Call me when you're done?"

"I will," said Jacob. "What time is it now?"

"It's three-fifteen."

"Shit! You have to go, because I need to hurry. Let me take care of everything here, and you go take care of things on your end," Jacob said as he started quickly walking up the stairs. After a few steps, he stopped and said, "Steph... Please be careful."

"I will, Jacob. I know you're not going to say it back, but I love you."

Stephanie walked out of the house, and as the door closed, Jacob said, "I love you, too."

Stephanie sat in her Jeep, and she cautiously looked around as she started a text message to Derrick. "**I know things are so fucked up between us right now, but you are in a lot of danger. Meet me for coffee at 8am, and I'll explain.**"

Derrick replied, "**If you're texting me at 4 in the morning, shit better be important.**"

"**Didn't you read my text? This is important!**"

"**Whatever... I'll meet you at 8.**"

Stephanie backed out of the driveway and drove off into the darkness of the early morning. As she looked at her home slowly shrinking through her rear-view mirror, she knew she could never go back there, and this was likely the last time she'd ever see the house. Her only thought was, *I guess I just lost my house, too - how the hell did all of this ever happen?*

• • •

Ten minutes before eight, Stephanie arrived at the coffee shop to wait for Derrick. She waited until almost eight-thirty before he finally strolled in. He looked like he just woke up as he pulled on the empty chair at her table and sat down. Stephanie had been up all night, and she looked every bit of it.

"You look like shit," said Stephanie as Derrick sat down.

Derrick quickly replied, "Obviously, there aren't any mirrors in your house." He sipped his coffee before continuing, "You called me here, so what's up?"

Stephanie glanced over her shoulders to be certain no one could overhear her conversation with Derrick, and she began, "My husband found out about us, and he left me."

"Yeah, so? That sounds like a Stephanie problem to me."

"God, you're an asshole. I'm actually trying to help you," said Stephanie. "And now, I'm starting to wonder why I am. It's going to become a Derrick problem really soon."

"How is it going to become my problem?"

"My husband has been following us around, and he knows who you are. Do you remember meeting a guy in a bar not long ago, and talking to him about the blonde and brunette you were *tapping*? Well, that was him."

"That guy was creepy as fuck – I knew something wasn't right with him. So he knows who I am, big deal."

"Derrick, I'm telling you, he's completely lost it I had a feeling he was going to want to do something to you, so last night I set a trap for him. I made up a story about wanting to get back at you, and he bought it. He told me all about what he's going to do to you, and it's not good."

Derrick, starting to take the conversation a little more seriously, asked, "And what exactly does he plan on doing?"

"He knows you park your motorcycle in the parking spot next to the alley behind your building. He's going to start following you and watching until you leave on your bike. Once you're gone, he's going to wait in the alley for you, and when you come back, he's going to make it look like a robbery that went bad."

"He's going to make what look like a robbery that went bad?"

"What do you think, asshole? He's going to kill you."

Derrick ran his fingers through his hair and took a deep breath which he slowly exhaled. He asked, "What's his deal? Is he a threat? He didn't look like much, but I learned a long time ago to never judge that kind of shit just by looking at someone."

"Honestly, I'm not sure. I don't think he's dangerous, but I don't think you can ever really know something like that."

Derrick asked, "Was he in the military?"

"Yes, he was in the Air Force," said Stephanie. "He was a fighter pilot in Afghanistan when the war first started, and then he taught some kind of school. I forget it was called sire school or something."

"Derrick knew what Stephanie meant, and he corrected her, "It's called *SERE* School, S-E-R-E, Survival Evasion

Resistance and Escape. And you're sure he taught SERE training?"

"Yes, he was an instructor there for his last two years."

"That could be a problem," Derrick said. "SERE training is actually some pretty badass shit. They teach fighter pilots how to survive through almost anything if they crash in enemy territory. The part I don't like, is they teach them how to keep from getting captured, including how to kill with almost anything."

"Oh my God, Derrick. I don't want him to hurt you."

"Why are you even telling me all this? What's in it for you?"

"Nothing's in it for me," said Stephanie. "I'm scared you're going to get hurt."

"Don't bullshit a bullshitter, Stephanie. You hate me, and I know you do. We both know you think I'm an asshole, so why are you really doing this?"

"Honestly? ...wait, forget I asked that," Stephanie said with a chuckle. "I'm telling you because there is a part of me that still wants to be with you. Don't ask me to explain why, because even I don't understand it. You have a hold on me, and I don't want you to let go."

"And what's in it for you?" Derrick asked suspiciously.

"Yes, what's in it for me?" Stephanie looked around again before she leaned in and quietly explained, "You're going to think I'm a cold-hearted bitch, but I just want Jacob gone. He has so much hanging over me that he's going to skin me alive in a divorce. He already took my car and left me with his shitty Jeep, and I know he's going to take everything else. If he's gone, well, he'll be gone and so will my worries."

"Yeah, you're right I think you're a cold-hearted bitch, and I also believe the second reason a lot more than the first, but either way, I have to do something about this. If I know exactly when he's coming, where he'll be, and what he's planning, it will be easy for me to make it look like self-defense. I can kill him right there in the alley, and it will be nice and clean. Can you find all of that out for me?"

"I will, in exchange for one thing...." said Stephanie.

"And here it comes," said Derrick. "I knew you were going to want something out of this."

"Let Karen go, and be done with her. Just let her walk away, don't hold anything over her anymore, and let her be free."

"Not going to happen," Derrick quickly snapped.

"Hold on, sparky. I'm not done yet. If you let Karen go, not only will I completely help you with Jacob, I'll also take her place."

"You'll take her place?" asked Derrick.

"Yes, I'll take her place. I know what I'll always be to you, nothing more than a toy, and I'm okay with it. The way you make me feel when you control me and have your way with me is beyond words. And I'm willing to accept that I'd never be anything more than just a little piece of trash to you. I only want to get to experience that same feeling you give me, over and over again."

"That sounds all well and good," said Derrick, "but I really pushed Karen hard. I made her do things that would definitely make you change your mind about this."

"Whatever it is you want, I'll do it. Make me your slave, baby. I'll be your obedient, naughty, kinky, filthy, little fuck-toy slave. I'll wear anything you tell me to, I'll do anything you say, and you can even bring home a different girl every other night and make me watch you fuck her - absolutely, one hundred percent no limits. Just let Karen go."

"I'll make a deal with you. I haven't heard from Karen since yesterday, and if I don't hear from her really soon, I'm going to start punishing that little bitch hard. But I'll hold off and wait to give you one shot. If you really want to do this for her, come back, and be ready for me to push you just as hard."

"Just tell me what to wear and when to show up, and I'll be here."

"What the hell day is it today?" Derrick said while yawning.

Stephanie was exhausted and confused as to what day it was herself, but after a second of thought, she replied, "It's Friday.

"I'm tied up this weekend with some stuff from work, but I'm free Monday night. Once you start this, you know I'm not going to let you stop, right? This isn't something you get to just walk away from when it becomes too much."

"I know, Derrick. I'm not going to want to walk away. I told you, I want to be your slave."

"I'm going to video you Monday night, and I'll make more videos as time goes on. If you ever try to walk, I'll show them to everyone you love."

"I know, and I'm not worried because I'm not going anywhere."

"Be back here at nine o'clock on Monday night," Derrick said as he was simultaneously typing on his phone. Without saying another word, he stood to his feet and walked away. He reached the door when Stephanie received a text from him stating, "**Use your imagination, and wear something that screams *slave.***"

● ● ●

Stephanie gathered her things and went shopping for clothes to wear over the next several days. She bought the essentials such as panties, bras, socks, and a few comfortable outfits. Her last stop was the lingerie shop near the District Attorney's Office.

"Hi, Amanda!" Stephanie said as she walked in and recognized the sales associate.

"Well, welcome back. Is there anything specific you're looking for today?"

"There is actually," said Stephanie. She was originally intending to shop by herself, but she figured Amanda may be able to help her pick out something more appropriate for the night. "My boyfriend and I are kind of experimenting with role playing, and I want something that will fit the bill for tonight's game."

"Naughty, naughty," said Amanda as she continued, "And what exactly is tonight's theme?"

Stephanie said, "Tonight, I'm his bad little slave."

"Total hotness," said Amanda while shooting Stephanie a smile and a wink. "I have just the perfect idea."

Amanda and Stephanie pieced together an assortment of different outfits and accessories until they found the perfect combination that was sure to please. Stephanie tried on the complete ensemble, and Amanda peeked her head into the fitting room.

"That is beyond hot," said Amanda.

"You think he'll like it?"

"Are you kidding me, sweetie? He's going to *love* it!"

Stephanie put her own clothes back on, brought her new accessories to the register, and handed Amanda her credit card as Amanda told her, "I hope someone has fun tonight."

Stephanie left the boutique and called Jacob. When he answered she asked, "I'm afraid to ask, but is everything taken care of at the house?"

Jacob paused and said, "Yes, everything is done. How are you doing?"

She said, "It's taking everything I have to stay focused and make it through the next few days. I'm holding it together for now, but I don't know how long it will last."

"Be strong, it's only going to be a few days, maybe a week at the most. After that, you can crash and fall apart all you want. What are you up to now?"

"I'm going to look for a hotel, and then I think I'm going to sleep for a month. Can I see you tonight?"

"We have to meet up for a little while tonight. I have a few things from the house I need to give you, and I have Karen's things. After that, I'll have to go."

"I know," said Stephanie. "I just wish I didn't have to stay in a hotel alone."

He replied, "Just go get a hotel, get in your room, and do nothing but sleep and order room service until we're ready to move on this; I'll stop by for a few minutes tonight. Have you talked to *him* yet?"

"I did, this morning. He wants to see me on Monday night."

"Monday night? Can't you get over there any earlier than that?"

"He said he had to work all weekend, and I didn't want to be pushy. This is getting dangerous, Jacob."

"I know it is, but shit, I needed you to get in there earlier than Monday. Okay, just do the best you can, and we're just going to have to adjust our plan as we go. Once you're checked into a hotel, let me know where you're staying, and we'll talk more then."

"Just promise me one thing?" asked Stephanie. "Please promise me you won't ever be far from me until this is over? I'll just feel safer if I know you're close by."

The lie burned Jacob's soul as he uttered the words, "I promise you, I won't let anything happen to you. I never would." He knew it was a promise he couldn't keep, because once she entered Derrick's apartment, everything was out of Jacob's hands.

The two said goodbye, and as they ended their phone call, Stephanie had the overwhelming desire to tell Jacob she loved him. And while she resisted the urge, Jacob was hoping to hear her say it.

Stephanie spent the afternoon looking for a hotel somewhere in the downtown area. Jacob had instructed Stephanie to find a cheap hotel, but she said *why the hell not?* when she found herself driving by the Boston Park Plaza Hotel. As she passed the hotel, she did a quick U-turn and drove to the valet drive-up. She carried her shopping bags filled with new clothes through the hotel's beautiful modern lobby. While she was waiting in line for the check-in desk, she messaged Jacob, "Boston Park Plaza Hotel. I'll get you the room number once I'm in."

Jacob replied, "So much for somewhere cheap. Try your best to take it easy and relax. I'll be there around seven thirty."

Once she was checked in to a room, Stephanie went straight to the bathroom where she started a piping hot bath. She drank from the bottle of tequila she purchased in the hotel's lobby gift shop, and she watched the steam rise from the bathwater as she stepped in and inched her body lower and lower into the tub. She tried to let her worries melt away as the hot water enveloped her body, and she pressed a warm washcloth over her eyes. All that was left to do now was wait.

• • •

Stephanie heard a knock on her hotel room door, and she looked through the peephole to see Jacob standing in the hall. "Come in, come in," she said as she opened the door.

Stephanie was wearing only a bath towel wrapped around her body, and Jacob asked, "Did I come at a bad time?"

"Not at all, she replied. Let me just run in the bathroom and get dressed." Once she was in the bathroom with the door closed, she continued her conversation with Jacob through the door, "So asshole wants me to wear something that screams 'slave' for him on Monday night."

"This guy is unreal," said Jacob.

"The worst part was going out today and picking out an outfit like that," Stephanie said as her voice echoed inside the bathroom.

Jacob felt crushed by Stephanie's comment as he didn't expect her to actually wear anything like that for Derrick again. He asked, "You actually bought something like that for him, today?"

The door opened, and Stephanie walked out while saying, "Not for him – I got it for you."

Stephanie walked toward Jacob who was sitting on the hotel bed. She was wearing black Taylor Reeve stiletto-pump heels with a red heart on the front, black fishnet stockings, a black form-fitting corset, and a black collar around her neck.

Jacob rose to his feet from the bed and told her, "Stephanie, we really shouldn't do this. It's a very bad idea."

Stephanie stared Jacob straight in the eye as she told him, "You're not going anywhere, and you're taking hold of me and using me in every way imaginable, tonight. I keep blaming myself for everything that's happened between us, but you, Mister, are just as responsible. I begged and begged for you to take me like this, and you pushed me away so much that I felt I had no choice but to go find it somewhere else. Does that make what I did okay? No, but it does lay some of the blame on you." Jacob was left speechless by the words coming from Stephanie's mouth, and she continued, "If you want to walk away, fine, so be it. But if we're going to break up, you're going to leave me with something to remember." as she lowered herself to her knees in front of Jacob.

Jacob ran his hand through Stephanie's hair, and she rubbed her hand up his thigh and over the bulge forming in his pants. She looked up from her kneeling position between the bed and the wall, and explained, "If I'm not going to be your wife anymore, you have no reason not to make me your whore."

Jacob felt Stephanie rubbing his cock through his pants, and he watched her pushing her ass outward so he could clearly see her amazing beauty as he looked down at her. He saw the muscles along her lower back strengthen to highlight the beautiful shape of her body. "I'd be lying if I said there wasn't a part of me that wanted to fuck you like crazy for what you did."

Stephanie cracked a seductive smile and said, "Then do it. Punish me, rip me apart, and make me pay, baby. I know you watch porn on your computer – I've seen your browser cache. Treat me like the girls in your videos, and make my cute little bum pay for what I did."

Jacob, wearing a pair of jeans, and an American Eagle T-shirt, undid his pants and started to lower them. Stephanie, like a shark who just smelled blood, pulled them down and she reached for his semi-hard cock. She grasped it in her hand and told Jacob, "We need to make this thing hard."

Jacob replied, "Then use your mouth for something other than talking."

Stephanie leaned in and wrapped her lips around his cock. As it was still somewhat flaccid, she was able to take him completely in, but her talented mouth quickly changed that. As her fingers massaged his balls, her lips wrapped tight, and her tongue swirled around the tip of his shaft, she felt him growing harder and harder until his throbbing cock was at its full size. Stephanie, unable to take him fully in her mouth at that point, was trying to deep throat him, but she could only take him barely more than three-quarters of the way. Jacob decided that wasn't enough.

He forcefully pushed her back so she fell to a seated position with her back against the wall. He stepped forward and pushed her head back against the wall so she could not pull back. He straddled her face and went back inside her mouth. He began pushing his way deeper and deeper as the head of his cock traveled down her throat. Stephanie's eyes watered as Jacob pushed beyond her gag point. Stephanie tried to pull back, but with her head against the wall, she had no choice but to take every inch until she felt his balls touching her lips. Jacob pulled his cock from her throat and out of her mouth, and Stephanie gasped for breath.

"Oh my God," gasped Stephanie.

Jacob placed the palm of his hand on her forehead and pressed her head back against the wall. He told her, "Open up," as he went back in for more, and he fucked her throat repeatedly, only occasionally stopping to give her a moment to catch her breath. Jacob let out a series of low moans as the muscles in Stephanie's throat tightened and squeezed around his cock.

Jacob reached down and looped his index and middle fingers through the collar around her neck, and he pulled her to her feet. As she stood up, Stephanie's eyes were watering with her makeup running, and a string of saliva running from her chin to her chest. Jacob's anger coupled with the intensity of the scenario allowed him to emotionally disconnect from his wife, and for the first time, he looked at her as a sexual object and not just the woman he was in love with. He decided it was time to turn it up a notch.

Stephanie reached her lips to kiss Jacob, but he pushed her back against the wall. He wrapped his left hand around her throat as he told her, "Whores don't get to kiss."

"Kiss me, baby. I want to taste your lips," begged Stephanie.

Jacob ignored her words and was entranced by her breasts bulging from the top of her black corset. His right hand grabbed the top of her left breast cup, and pulled down to expose her luscious breast. The index finger and thumb on his right hand formed a vice-like grip on her nipple, and he began to twist while simultaneously applying more pressure to her throat with his left hand. "Do you deserve to be kissed?" he asked as he twisted her nipple again.

Stephanie replies, "Not me! Not me!"

"And why not?"

"Because whores don't deserve to be kissed, but they do deserve to be fucked," she answered.

Jacob grabbed her and spun her around, pressing her chest into the wall. He grabbed her hips, pulling her ass outward while her face and chest remained pressed against the wall. He shredded his clothes off, and he began rubbing the tip of his cock over her wet pussy. He slid his cock under her, and he rubbed the top of his shaft back and forth over her clit, making her groan with delight. Once his cock was covered with the fluid pouring from within her, Jacob forced his way into her pussy as she let out an uncontrolled, "Fuck yes!"

He started fucking her from behind and unclasping her corset until it peeled from her body and fell you the floor. She felt his hands holding her hips while his balls slapped against her pussy with each powerful slam. His hand grabbed the back of her hair and controlled her against the wall while his cock made her pussy swell. Out of nowhere, Jacob placed his hands on her ribs just under her arms, picked her up, and threw her to the bed. She quickly rolled to her back, and scooted her ass to the edge of the mattress. As she was laying back, her arm reached behind her and moved the bottle of tequila from under her.

Jacob grabbed the tequila from Stephanie's hand and untwisted the cap. She was laying back on the bed, propped up on her elbows, and watching as Jacob brought the mouth of the open bottle towards her chest. He began pouring the liquor on her breasts and feverishly licking it off. His lips and tongue focused extra attention on her nipples as he licked and sucked them, sending chills down her spine. He then poured a splash on her stomach and showed her belly button the same attention he showed her tender, pink nipples.

His mouth and tongue wandered lower and lower until they were at the very start of her pussy. She groaned, "Please tell me that a bad little whore gets to have her pussy eaten!?!"

The residue of alcohol on Jacob's tongue caused a slight burning sensation on Stephanie's pussy as his tongue made its first pass. The burning quickly subsided and was replaced by the euphoric sensation of Jacob's crafty tongue pleasing her. His tongue swirled in a plethora of patterns, on and around her clit, causing her body to convulse closer and closer to orgasm.

"Oh God, Jacob," Stephanie moaned. "If you make me cum, I'll do anything you want. Don't stop and I'll let you fuck my ass, cum in my face, slap me -- I'll do anything."

Jacob only pressed his tongue harder against her, and he went until her back arched, her legs began to shake, and she exploded into beautiful orgasm. He stood up and said, "My turn," as he stood next to the bed, held her legs up, and went back to fucking her.

Within a minute or two of being back inside her, Stephanie blurted out, "I want to taste my pussy on you, baby," as she pulled away and swung herself around. She positioned herself so she was laying on her stomach with her face right at the edge of the bed. With her mouth being at the perfect level for Jacob to assault her with another intense face-fucking, he grabbed her hair to pull her head up, and he inserted his hard cock back into her hot mouth. Stephanie bent her knees, kicking her heeled feet into the air, and she reached back with both hands to grab hold of the heels of her shoes while Jacob rammed her throat. One of his hands was pulling her hair, and his other hand was wrapped around her throat, while she felt Jacob having the time of his life.

Jacob pulled away, and ordered Stephanie to roll to her hands and knees. Stephanie reached her right hand across her back, she looked back at Jacob, and she began running her index finger over her tight ass. "This is what I want, baby, right in here," she said as she pressed the tip of her finger into her asshole.

"I want to watch you," Jacob replied.

"Anything you want," Stephanie said as she lowered her shoulders to the bed. She reached between her legs with her left hand, and Jacob started stroking his cock as he watched Stephanie fingering herself. The fingers on her left hand were working her pussy, and her right index finger was sliding in and out of her ass. Jacob started to throb as he saw her add her middle finger, and she used two fingers to fuck her own ass.

"Do you like making me do this?" Stephanie asked.

"I fucking love it!"

"Good, baby. I'll do anything for you," Stephanie moaned. "Just promise me that you'll cum all over my little whore face, tonight."

"If that's what you want, then you better come get it."

Jacob grabbed the bottle of tequila again and poured some on his tall-standing cock. Stephanie rushed to her knees and told him, "Mmmmm, my favorite shot!" She looked up and said, "Just watch me. Let me finish you, but tell me when you're going to cum."

She started devouring and stroking his cock, sucking her cheeks in and swirling her tongue as she went. She swiped some of the saliva running down her chin to the fingers on her free hand, and she used those dripping fingers to play with his balls and the area just behind them. His moans and grunts told her he was loving everything she was doing. The sound of her mouth sucking and the slobbering sound of her hand stroking his saliva drenched shaft combined to create the most erotic noise for Jacob.

To Stephanie's surprise, however, he suddenly pulled away from her and pushed her to the floor. He told her to lay on her back, and he climbed on top of her, straddling her midsection with his knees on either side of her ribs. He placed his cock between her breasts, and Stephanie used both hands to push on her tits and wrap them around him. He started gliding his cock back and forth, and as Jacob was fucking her tits, she raised her head off the floor and licked the tip of his cock with each pass as it came at her.

"Fuck my tits, baby. Fuck my tits until you cum!"

She knew she had finally unlocked his inner animal when he uttered, "Look up at me," and as she did, he continued, "Point it at your face - jerk me off all over your face!"

More than happy to oblige, Stephanie pulled his cock from between her tits and started stroking. She laid her head back, closed her eyes, and pumped her hand until she felt streams of Jacob's cum splattering her face until the warm fluid ran down her neck and onto her tits.

Ten minutes later, they were in the shower together, washing one another. "I can't believe how hot that was. That was better than anything I ever imagined," Jacob said with immense excitement.

"You see, dummy! That's what I wanted. That's what I've been wanting for so long. Why didn't you just do this a long time ago?"

"Because I was an idiot. I got too comfortable, and I thought you'd never leave. I stopped paying attention a long time ago, and I fucked up. I fucked up big time." He looked at Stephanie and asked, "So, where do we go from here?"

"Are you still leaving me?" she asked. "Because you don't have to."

"Two hours ago, I was completely certain what I needed to do. Now, I have no idea what the hell's going to happen. The only thing I do know is that not having you is killing me."

Stephanie suggested, "Then let's not decide on anything right now. Let's just get through this weekend, and once this is all over, we'll figure everything out from there, with one hundred percent no pressure. Sound good?"

"Sounds perfect," Jacob said as he kissed her on the forehead.

"Sounds perfect to me, too," Stephanie said with a happy sigh.

● ● ●

12

Best Served Cold

The weekend crept by at a snail's pace, and Stephanie was going stir crazy with anxiety until Monday evening was finally upon her. She called Jacob and told him she was getting ready to go to Derrick's apartment, and he told her he had rented a car so he could follow her to Derrick's without the risk of being spotted.

Stephanie asked Jacob, "Are you positive you can promise me it will happen tonight?"

"I promise you, it will. It's definitely happening tonight, but you need to get in there and then back out as soon as you can."

"And you promise me I'll never have to go back in there after this?" Stephanie impatiently asked. "Whatever you need him to do, I can get him to do it, tonight. Please,

Jacob, I need this to be over. I don't think I can handle this anymore."

"It will be soon, sweetheart, it's almost over. After tonight, you'll never have to go back again."

Stephanie developed a gentle knot in her throat as she pointed out, "You just called me *sweetheart*. I love when you call me that."

"You are my sweetheart," said Jacob. " But you need to stay focused. Just remember two things: the most important thing is for you to be careful tonight. No matter what happens, I couldn't live with myself if anything happened to you. The second thing you cannot forget is to keep your phone near you. Did you change my name in your contacts?"

"I changed your name to Jillian."

"Okay, and what's the code?" he quizzed Stephanie.

She answered, "Are you free for lunch tomorrow?"

"Perfect! If you get a text from me asking if you're free for lunch tomorrow, get your ass out of there fast."

"Why can't you come pick me up and bring me yourself?" asked Stephanie. "I can't be alone anymore – I feel like I'm losing it."

"You know we can't run the risk of him seeing us together near his apartment. I can't be one hundred percent sure that he hasn't been watching you, so we can't take that chance. I don't know how smart or how stupid this guy really is, so I can't put it past him."

"Can you at least tell me what kind of car you're going to be in, so I can look to see you when I get there?"

"No, I can't, Steph. If you know what kind of car I'm in, you might look at me, and he might see you looking. You need to trust me that I'm covering every base here, but you also need to trust me that I will be there. You won't see me, but I'll see you every step of the way."

"I completely trust you," said Stephanie. She paused for a moment before working up the courage to ask, "Jacob?"

"Yeah, Steph?"

She said, "I just...." but stopped after not having the strength to say the words if Jacob wasn't going to say them back.

Jacob quickly replied, "I love you, too, Stephanie. Now, let's go." as he ended the call.

Stephanie sat on the plush comforter on the hotel bed. She held the phone in her hand and looked down for a moment before texting Derrick, **"I don't think he plans on doing it tonight."**

• • •

Wearing dark gray yoga pants, a gray sweatshirt, tennis shoes, and clutching a small boutique bag, Stephanie walked along the brightly lit sidewalk adjacent to the north side of Boston Common, as she approached the coffee shop just a few minutes before nine. She saw Derrick walking from his building, and she shouted, "Derrick, I'm over here," as she waved to him.

Stephanie looked around for any sign of Jacob, but she had no idea what kind of car he would be driving. She quickly studied the cars parked along the street, looking for even the slightest indication of one being a rental, but none of the cars caught her attention. *Come on Jacob, where are you? You have to be here.*

Derrick asked her, "Worried about tonight?"

"A little anxious, but not worried."

"You should be worried," he replied with a malevolent tone. "And what's up with the outfit? It doesn't exactly look like what I was expecting."

Stephanie held up the boutique bag and said, "I couldn't exactly wear this in public."

"Fair enough," he replied. "Let me have a peek."

The two stopped, and Stephanie opened the bag. Derrick saw the heels and assorted pieces of lingerie and said, "I like it. What's this?" as he reached in the bag and pointed out a plastic freezer storage bag. Stephanie moved some of the contents in the boutique bag to show him several pairs of stockings in the freezer bag.

"I liked the way you used lingerie to tie me up last time, so I brought a whole bunch," she said while raising her eyebrow at him.

"What? Do you think that you're going to get brownie points for coming prepared?" he asked while groping her ass through her tight pants on the busy city sidewalk.

"No, I just thought..."

He said, "You don't need to think, tonight. Just do what I tell you to do," and pushed her forward. "Let's get upstairs."

As they rode the elevator, Derrick asked, "Any word on the thing with your husband?"

"I talked to him earlier, and he still thinks I'm helping him get to you. He has no idea I'm telling you everything. From what he said, he's going to be outside here, but it doesn't sound like he's going to be waiting for you tonight."

"When he *isn't* going to be waiting for me isn't very helpful. When *is* he going to be waiting for me?" Derrick nervously asked.

"I have no idea, but I know he'll tell me as soon as he plans on doing it. He thinks I'm going to help him by telling him when you'll be going out to the alley. I'll tell you the second I know something."

"And it's definitely not tonight?"

For the first time since meeting him, Stephanie saw tremendous weakness in Derrick as his fear of Jacob was evident in his string of questions. She answered, "It's definitely not tonight."

The two reached Derrick's door, and he asked her, "Once you walk in there, there's no walking out until I'm done. If you do this, I own your ass."

"You give me your word that Karen is free if I do?"

"You have my word, cross my heart," Derrick said as he made an x motion across his chest with his fingers.

She took a deep breath and said, "Let's go in."

They walked through the door to Derrick's apartment, and he instructed her to go in his bedroom and change. She asked, "Are you going to hurt me tonight?"

"Yes," he answered. "Tonight is going to be very painful."

"Can you make me one of your drinks while I change? Something to make it just a little easier for me."

"I guess I'll be a nice guy and do that for you."

"Thank you," she said. As she walked to the bedroom, she finished, "Your slave is very appreciative."

As soon as Stephanie closed the bedroom door, she placed her ear against it and listened until she was certain Derrick was in the kitchen. She could hear the sound of the glass crushing the pills on the granite counter top, and she hurried to open her bag. She took out the plastic freezer bag and opened it to remove a cell phone hidden among the stockings. Stephanie glanced around the room as if she were looking for something. She saw a small pile of dirty clothes in the rear corner and she quickly hid the phone within the pile.

While Derrick was waiting for Stephanie on his living room couch, the bedroom door opened, and Stephanie emerged wearing the same yoga pants and sweatshirt she was wearing when she walked in. "Is there a problem?" he asked.

"I'm not comfortable with this anymore, Derrick. I can't go through with it."

"You can't go through with what exactly?" he asked as he was becoming obviously angry.

"This, you, all of it. I can't play your games anymore. I'm done with you." Stephanie said and started walking to the front door to leave.

As she was passing Derrick, she felt him grab her tight ponytail and pull back with enough force to make her fall to the floor. Stephanie crashed to the ground and yelled out in pain. She started to get up when Derrick yelled, "Where the fuck do you think you're going?"

He grabbed her hair with one hand and the hood of her sweatshirt with the other, and he dragged her into his bedroom. He pushed her to the ground next to her boutique bag, rolled her to her stomach, and sat on her back. As Derrick was sitting on Stephanie to hold her down, he rifled through the freezer bag to pull out a handful of the stockings. He pulled both of her arms behind her back and quickly bound her wrists together. Using a second stocking, he tied her ankles, and said, "I told you, you go when I say you can go. You're done when I tell you you're done, and you're not even close to walking out of here."

Stephanie cried, "Please, Derrick, please don't do this. I'm so scared."

Derrick walked out of the room and to the glass coffee table in his living room. He picked up a small video recorder from the table and began walking back to Stephanie. The contents of her purse had spilled across the floor from being thrown, and Derrick saw her cell phone alerting to an incoming text message. He picked up the phone and yelled to Stephanie, "Your friend Jillian wants to know if you're free for lunch tomorrow. Want me to tell her that you're probably not going to be up for it?" as he laughed.

"Derrick, you have to let me go. I don't want to do this," Stephanie pleaded as he walked in with the camera recording. He focused the video on her hysterically crying face as she begged.

"You see, that's where you're wrong, Princess. I don't have to let you go, and I'm not going to. In fact, I plan on having a lot of fun with you tonight. You, on the other hand, I don't think you're going to be having too much fun."

Derrick reached his hand into the back of Stephanie's yoga pants and he pulled violently, ripping her pants down, almost to her knees, while holding the recording camera with his free hand. Derrick rolled Stephanie to her back and crouched next to her.

"So, it looks like you don't want to cooperate tonight, but that's okay. I have the cure for that. He placed the camera on the floor and removed a tube of lipstick from his pocket. "Look what I found from the pile of shit that fell from your purse," as he showed her the lipstick. He removed the cap, twisted the tube, and grabbed Stephanie by the hair. He used the bright red lipstick to write *SLUT* across her forehead as she whimpered incoherently.

He pushed her back to her stomach as he stood and continued, "That's to remind you of what you are. I just don't like that you can easily wipe it off and forget, so I'm going to put something on you that you can't wipe off."

Derrick slid his belt from his waist and folded it in half. He trained the video camera on Stephanie as his hand pulled back and jerked the belt forward, sending a welting slap across her lower legs. Stephanie screamed in pain, and Derrick reached back to strike again. "Oh, you are in for a world of hurt, you stupid bitch," he said as he prepared to hit her again. "You might want to bite down on something."

Crack! Snapped the leather belt against Stephanie's soft skin. Derrick unloaded lash after lash of his belt against the back of her legs, her ass, and her lower back as she wailed in agony.

"Please, Derrick! Please, I'm begging you to please stop!" She cried.

Derrick's hand reached down and grabbed the back of Stephanie's pink lace thong. He pulled harder and harder, causing a ripping sound as he tore her panties off of her. The fabric painfully dug into her skin with each pull until they finally broke free.

Derrick rolled her torn and tattered underwear into a ball and stuffed them into Stephanie's mouth. He told her, "This ought to shut you up!"

Derrick stood back over Stephanie, and he looked at the rapidly swelling welts left by his belt. He snickered while he started unbuttoning his pants, and he said, "You might want to go to your happy place right about now."

As Stephanie attempted to mentally prepare herself for whatever horror she was to face next, she heard an explosion from Derrick's front door. The thunderous boom rocked through the entire apartment, and Derrick yelled, "What the fuck!"

Within a second, the apartment filled with yelling, "BOSTON POLICE WITH A SEARCH WARRANT! BOSTON POLICE WITH A SEARCH WARRANT!"

A S.W.A.T. team flowed into the apartment and the lead Officer raced toward the rear bedroom. Derrick saw the large officer, dressed in all black tactical gear, coming towards him while carrying a large assault rifle.

The Officer yelled, "BOSTON P.D. GET ON THE FUCKING GROUND, NOW!"

Derrick hesitated a moment longer than the officer was willing to allow, and the officer drove the butt of his rifle to the side of Derrick's head, immediately dropping him to the floor stunned and nearly unconscious.

Stephanie felt a police officer's hand on her shoulder and the blade of his knife between her wrists. The knife began slicing through the stocking being used to bind her as he told her, "Just hold still. You're safe, now."

The officer then cut the stocking from her ankles and helped her to pull her pants up as she rolled to her side. Stephanie reached to her face to wipe the lipstick writing from her forehead as she said, "Thank you. Thank you, so much. I thought I was going to die in here."

"I think you might be right, ma'am." Said the officer while stopping her from wiping her forehead. "You need to leave that there for just a few more minutes. We need to have someone take a picture of it for evidence. Is that okay with you?"

"Yes, just please hurry -- this is so humiliating."

"Don't be embarrassed, ma'am. None of this is your fault."

As Derrick was being handcuffed, and officers were tending to Stephanie, Jacob was at the front door of the apartment pleading with an officer, "My wife's in there, you have to let me in."

The officer replied, "Sir, this residence is a crime scene you can't come in," while pushing Jacob back.

Jacob suddenly saw Stephanie running to him from within the apartment while yelling, "Jacob!" She burst past the officer posted by the door and into Jacob's arms.

"It's over, baby. It's all over. I have you now, and I'm never letting go. Do you hear that? I'm never letting go."

Jacob held Stephanie up as he felt her body collapse. She tried to speak, but her crying made nearly all the words flowing across her tongue completely incomprehensible. "Oh my God, I love you," was all Jacob could make out.

● ● ●

Derrick sat alone in a small interrogation room at Boston Police Headquarters. The room was painted a pale blue color, and the only furnishings were a small table with a chair on either side. He looked at the large mirror on one side of the wall, and assuming someone was watching him from the other side, he shouted, "Are you dickheads coming in here soon or what?"

A moment later, a gruff, overweight Detective in his late forties walked into the room. He was wearing a white short-sleeve shirt with a very loose fitting tie, and he introduced himself, "I'm Detective Carter, and you are?"

"Pissed," Derrick replied as he pressed an ice pack against the large lump on his head.

Detective Carter sat across the small table from Derrick, and he peered over the top of his reading glasses as he replied, "There's two ways we can do this son, and the easy way doesn't have anything to do with you being a smart ass. What's your fucking name?"

"Derrick Hanson," he replied. "And when I get out of here, I'm suing the shit out of all of you people."

"I wouldn't go spending that big lawsuit money just yet if I were you," said the Detective.

"The girl in my apartment, Stephanie, she wanted to be there. She was there on her own. She came up there knowing damn well what was going to happen."

"Well, unfortunately for you, she's down the hall telling a very different story. I also saw a video you were making that sure doesn't look like she wanted to be there. In fact, I'll quote, '*Derrick, you have to let me go. I don't want to do this,*' is exactly what she said on the video."

Derrick angrily replied, "That shit is so out of context. Have fun trying to get anywhere with that."

Detective Carter said, "Let's just set that issue aside, because to be honest, that's really the least of your problems right now. We'll get back to it, though. For now, just tell me about your relationship with Karen Borden."

"Who?"

"Your girlfriend, Karen. You had a relationship with her, right?"

Derrick stumbled for an answer, "I mean, I know her, but barely. I know who she is, and that's about it."

"So, you only knew her a little? She was an acquaintance, someone you knew in passing?"

"Why do you keep referring to her in the past tense?" Derrick asked. "Is she okay?"

"No, she's not okay, she's actually dead. But the fact that she's dead is of less interest to me than how she got to be that way," Detective Carter coldly stated.

● ● ●

Four Nights Earlier:

Stephanie and Jacob had just walked into their house after discussing their plan to stage Karen's suicide as a murder. They had fine-tuned the necessary details to convincingly lead the police to the conclusion that it was Derrick who was responsible for her death.

They stood on the stairway talking until Stephanie said, "You're right, I'm just going to leave. Call me when you're done?"

"I will," said Jacob. "What time is it now?"

"It's three-fifteen."

"Shit! You have to go, because I need to hurry. Let me take care of everything here, and you go take care of things on your end," Jacob said as he started quickly walking up the stairs. After a few steps, he stopped and said, "Steph... Please be careful."

"I will, Jacob. I know you're not going to say it back, but I love you."

Stephanie walked out of the house, and as the door closed, Jacob said, "I love you, too."

Jacob climbed the stairs, and he paused with a feeling of anxiety as he stood at the doorway to the bedroom. Karen's upper body was obscured by the doorjamb, but he could see her legs extending outward from the closet. He took several deep breaths as he thought, *You have to do this, Jacob, you have to do this*. He took one last breath and said to himself, "Here we go."

He entered the room, and Karen's lifeless body came into full view as he walked in. Her face was a pale gray color, her lips had turned a dark shade of blue, and her now clouded eyes had the dark spots of petechial hemorrhaging which occurs during strangulation or hanging.

Jacob reached into the closet, with socks over his hands to avoid leaving his fingerprints, and he unbuckled the belt from the garment rod. He then placed the belt around Karen's neck and rolled her body onto her stomach. Jacob knew the internal injuries to the neck and throat of the victim of a hanging are much different than the injuries sustained by strangulation, and he needed to replicate the latter. He placed his knee in the back of her neck, and he began to forcefully pull back on the belt until he felt her throat crushing. He pulled and tore at her shirt to cause rips and strains in the fabric to indicate a struggle. Lastly, he pulled her hands behind her back and bound her wrists together with a plastic wire-tie to complete the illusion of

Karen being murdered rather than having taken her own life.

"I'm so sorry for this. I am just so sorry," he said, with a single tear rolling down his cheek, as he finished the gruesome task and stood to his feet.

Karen's petite size and very light weight made easy work of carrying her down the stairs and out to the car, and Jacob worried immensely as he made the short dash from his front door to the trunk of the Volvo parked in his driveway. He previously opened the trunk before bringing her body out, and although he saw no one outside at the time, he was terrified someone would witness him carrying the body. The transfer was completed without detection, however, and he made the forty-five minute drive from the house to Derrick's apartment building.

Jacob rushed to get to Derrick's before sunrise, and he arrived with mere minutes to spare. He drove to the rear of the building and slowly traveled through the back alley adjacent to the building. As he reached the mid-way point of the alley, he could clearly see the entrance at both ends. He left the engine running as he casually walked to the trunk, opened the lid, and took one last look around before hastily pulling Karen from the trunk. He momentarily cradled her in his arms as he brought her to the edge of the alley, and dropped her next to a pile of debris and rubbish. Jacob took one last look around, assuring no one had seen him, and rushed back into his car to make his getaway.

Karen stayed there, with the belt left around her neck, until she was discovered later in the morning, and there was nothing left to indicate it was Jacob who was responsible for disposing of her body.

Jacob drove to a local convenience store and he used cash to purchase a cheap, pay-as-you-go, disposable phone. He also purchased a minutes card so he could use it without the phone being linked or traced back to him in any way. After the temporary account was activated, he initiated the only call the phone would ever be used to make.

"Boston Police Communications Center, Johnson speaking, how can I help you?"

"Yes, can I talk to a Homicide Detective, please?" asked Jacob.

"If you need to report a homicide, sir, you need to hang up and dial nine-one-one."

"No, I'm not reporting a murder; I have information, and I need to speak with someone."

"Please hold," said the operator.

The phone rang for a moment before being answered, "Homicide," by a man with a very disinterested tone.

Jacob explained, "I know this is going to sound shitty, but I saw something that I don't want to get involved in, but I feel like I have to say something. Are you the person I should talk to?"

The man on the other end of the phone sarcastically replied, "Sir, how can I know if I'm the person you need to talk to if I have no idea what you're even talking about."

Jacob explained, "I think I saw a murder last night, or at least part of one, anyway. At first I shrugged it off thinking I must have been mistaken and didn't see what I thought I was seeing. I've been thinking about it all day, playing it over and over again in my mind, and now I'm certain of what I saw. I know I should have called last night, but I need to tell someone about it."

"I'm the person you need to talk to," the man said. "Can I just get your name please?"

"No, I'm not comfortable giving my name. I don't want to get involved any more than this, but I'll tell you what I saw if you think it might help you."

"Okay, go ahead."

"I was cutting through an alley just north of The Common, around one in the morning, and I saw a guy pulling something out of the trunk of his car. At first I didn't think anything of it, but as I was driving right by him, I'm almost sure it was a woman he was pulling out."

"What makes you say that?" asked the man.

"I think I saw blonde hair."

"Are you sure there's no way I can get you to talk to me in person?" asked the man on the phone. "I think that would really be best."

Jacob said, "There's no way I'm getting involved in this. I'll hang up, right now, and never call back if I think you're going to push me into something."

"Not at all, sir. Just keep telling me what you saw — what did this guys look like?"

"It was so quick. I just remember he was a white guy, maybe in his early thirties, and he had a goatee."

"Great, great, is there anything else you can tell me about him?"

"Tattoos," said Jacob. "He had a lot of tattoos on his forearms."

"What kind of car was he taking her out of, do you remember?"

Jacob remained silent before saying, "A BMW. It was a black BMW."

"I just need to ask you," the man started asking before Jacob interrupted.

"Was there a murder? Did I really see what I think I saw?"

"Why do you ask that?"

"I have to go," Jacob said as he ended the call.

Jacob got out of his Volvo and wiped down the phone with a rag, to remove any fingerprints, and he threw the phone in a nearby trashcan on the sidewalk. His own phone vibrated, and he looked at the screen to see that it was Stephanie calling. He answered to hear Stephanie ask him, "I'm afraid to ask, but is everything taken care of at the house?"

Jacob paused and answered, "Yes, everything is done. How are you doing?"

● ● ●

Still in the interrogation room with Detective Carter, Derrick exclaimed, "Holy shit, man! Alright, I didn't have shit to do with anything that might have happened to her, so I'm going to be completely honest."

"That would be lovely."

"I've been dating her for a couple of years, but I didn't want to say anything because she's married. We have a sexual relationship, and that's it. Nothing more and nothing less. I didn't have shit to do with anything that could have hurt her."

Detective Carter let out a long exhale, and said, "That's not how I'm seeing it. Just be honest with me. Did you two have a fight? Were you upset that Karen was breaking up with you? If you just snapped and something happened, we can work with that, but you have to talk to me."

"I didn't do anything to her - I swear on my fucking mother!"

Detective Carter compassionately said, "Derrick, I want to help you, but you need to help me to help you. You need to tell me what happened, and we can fix it. We just need to know exactly what happened."

"I'm not a god damned moron," said Derrick. "You're not going to buddy up to me and get me to admit to something I didn't do." He stared up at the ceiling and said, "I think I need a lawyer. When they first brought me in here, they read me my rights, and they said I could have a lawyer before I talk to you. I want one."

"Sounds like a good idea, but just remember something: if you cooperate and work with me, you only make it easier on yourself in the end." Detective Carter leaned in, bringing his nose to within an inch of Derrick's. Derrick could smell the mixture of coffee and cigarettes on the Detective's breath as he continued, "But if you fuck with me, I promise you'll spend the rest of your life rotting in a maximum security prison."

"I want a lawyer," said Derrick.

"Alright, tough guy. I won't ask you anything else, but you don't need a lawyer to listen. So I'll tell you what you're up against, and then you decide if you still want a lawyer, okay?"

"Whatever."

"Tonight, you're being charged with First Degree Premeditated Murder, Kidnapping, False Imprisonment, Sexual Battery, Extortion, and Battery."

"Hold on, wait," said Derrick. "I didn't kill anyone. I didn't do any of that."

"Then why did Karen disappear? She called in sick to work on Thursday morning, and no one has seen her since."

"I don't know," said Derrick. "I was with her on Thursday, but she left, and she was fine. We had a fight later on, because I was also hooking up with her friend, but it was only by text. I never saw her after she left"

Detective Carter opened a file folder and ran his finger down a page until stopping, and he asked "Is that when you told her, and I'm quoting, 'I'm going to destroy you, you stupid bitch. You and your little fucking friend?' We subpoenaed her cell phone records, and we have transcripts of every text conversation you ever had with her. You were tormenting the shit out of this girl."

"That's not what it looks like!" yelled Derrick.

"Is that the last time you talked to her?"

"Yes. She left, we fought by text, and that was it. I said some shit that I probably shouldn't have, and I haven't seen her or heard from her since."

"If you didn't see her again after this text message was sent, then how exactly did her phone, the same phone she was texting you from, get back in your apartment *after* you had this conversation with her? How is that possible?"

"It couldn't have been in my apartment, I haven't seen her since then."

"We have Detectives ripping your place apart, and they found her phone in the laundry pile in your bedroom."

Derrick, knowing full well he never had Karen's phone, began to think the information was a bluff, and he decided to call it. "Yeah, you found her phone?" he asked in his typical arrogant tone. "If you found her phone, then show it to me."

Detective Carter laughed and said, "I don't have to show you shit. The ball is in my court, son, and I make the rules."

"Yeah, dickhead? What puts the ball in your court?"

"You want to know what puts the ball in my court? The fact that you get into a fight with your married girlfriend, you tell her you're going to destroy her, and she goes missing that same night -- that's a good start. Then her phone magically appears back in your apartment after you have this fight with her, and your only explanation is the cell phone fairy must have brought it -- that's pretty good, too. I think we're definitely getting warmer, but you want to know the best part? We found her body in the alley behind *your* apartment with a belt around her neck -- and guess whose fingerprints were all over the belt buckle? Yours!"

"I didn't kill her!" screamed Derrick.

"I'm not even done yet, you arrogant son of a bitch. The icing on the cake is when the S.W.A.T. team kicks in your door to go get you, and they find you in the middle of raping and beating the shit out of a woman in your bedroom, and with a belt no less. So, if you want to keep up this *I didn't do it* bullshit, be my guest, but just be ready to face a very painful truth. You're not the kind of guy that does well in prison, and I can only go out on a limb and assume that you're going to have a very, very hard time in there."

Derrick felt the room spinning as he was overcome with the confusion of not understanding anything that was happening to him. He quickly lurched to his left side and violently threw up on the floor. "I didn't kill Karen," he groaned as the wafting smell of vomit filled the room.

"Have your lawyer argue that one for you, son," said Detective Carter as he got up and walked out of the room.

In a separate interrogation room down the hall, Stephanie finished providing her statement to Detectives, and Bill Webber was sitting in. As she concluded, Webber asked, "My God, Bradford, why didn't you ever tell me? You know I would have done anything to help you girls."

"We were so scared, Bill. We were so scared he was going to kill us if we said anything, and we were right. The day I told him I'd had enough, Karen was dead."

"Listen, Bradford. I can't get you your job back, but it is very important for you to be willing to testify against this monster. A big part of getting a conviction on this is going to be your testimony. If you're willing to do that, I can arrange to have your DUI and Possession charge thrown out."

"Can you get the charge expunged and the record sealed?" asked Stephanie while sniffling through tears.

Webber stood next to Stephanie, placed his hand on her shoulder and said, "Expunged and sealed, absolutely."

"Bill, I'm so sorry about everything," said Stephanie as she stood up and hugged him.

"Don't be sorry. Never regret anything, just always remember to move forward."

"I will, I'll keep moving forward."

"And Bradford, one last thing. I was talking to your husband while I was waiting to come in and speak with you. He's a good man, and he really loves you. I know you two have a lot of issues to work through, and it's definitely not going to be easy, but don't ever stop loving that man. I know he's never going to stop loving you."

"I don't know where my life goes from here, Bill, but one thing I do know for sure, without even the slightest doubt, is that I will never stop loving him with every ounce of who I am."

Webber walked Stephanie out to the station's main lobby where she saw Jacob waiting for her. He held two cups in his hand, and he handed one to her, "I got you a hot chocolate."

"I don't want a hot chocolate," she said. "I want you, Jacob. You're all I ever wanted. Can we go home?"

"Where is home going to be?" Jacob asked. "You know we can't go back to the house."

"Home isn't a place, Jacob, it's a feeling. As long as I'm with you, I'm home. Can I please come home?"

"I think we both need you to come home," answered Jacob.

• • •

Shortly after Derrick was arrested, Bill Webber tragically passed away from a sudden heart attack at home. Eighteen months passed, and Stephanie kept the promise she made to Webber, and she continued to move forward with her life. She never stopped looking at him as a mentor, even though he was gone, and she worked to model her own life after the fine example he set.

Due to his death, Webber wasn't able to oversee the prosecution of Derrick Hanson, but the trial was essentially a slam dunk. Between the crime scene Jacob created by dumping Karen's body behind Derrick's building, the Medical Examiner testifying that it was Derrick's belt that was used to either strangle or hang Karen, the threatening and violent text messages sent by Derrick, Karen's cell phone being found in his apartment, and the convincing testimony concocted by Stephanie, it took a jury of his peers only one hour to unanimously agree to convict Derrick. He was sentenced to serve three consecutive life sentences at the Cedar Junction Maximum Security Men's Correctional Facility in Walpole, Massachusetts, and he would never be eligible for parole.

Stephanie was able to have her criminal charges dropped in exchange for testifying in court, and she did have her record sealed, but the Massachusetts Bar Association was notified of her arrest. They suspended her law license for a period of six months, and because of this, she was unable to find a job as an attorney even after the suspension period ended. She was, however, hired to work as a legal assistant in the Public Defender's Office, and she refuses to give up the dream of one day returning to the District Attorney's Office again as a State Prosecutor.

After all they had been through, and the dark secret they shared, Stephanie and Jacob decided to take things slowly. They thought it would be best to go back to square one and somewhat date again before making any long term decisions. That lasted all of three weeks, and before they knew it, they were living together in Jacob's new apartment. The two vowed never again to take the other for granted, and although it took Jacob a long time to move beyond what had happened, they walked away from the experience stronger and more devoted than ever. They eventually bought a new home together, one with new memories and a new start, and Stephanie really had moved forward with her life.

On a bright, sunny, Saturday morning, Stephanie walked to their new kitchen to start the coffee maker and pour a bowl of cereal for herself. The phone rang, and she answered to be greeted by a Facility Director from the Massachusetts Department of Corrections.

Jacob walked into the kitchen to see a look of utter shock on her face. He repeatedly asked who she was talking to while she listened intently to the caller, and she waved Jacob off, indicating she couldn't interrupt her conversation.

"I understand. Thank you very much for calling," said Stephanie. After a pause during which the caller was speaking, she concluded the conversation, " I will be sure to, and thank you again. I truly appreciate you letting me know."

She hung up the phone and stood silent for a moment, with Jacob again asking who was on the phone. "Stephanie, what's wrong? Who was that?"

"It's done, Jacob. It's all done."

"What's done?" Jacob asked, concerned by Stephanie's dazed demeanor.

"All of it -- it's finally all over."

● ● ●

Epilogue

Two days earlier, Derrick was working his assigned job in the prison laundry when a guard came in and instructed all the inmates to leave the area. Derrick was doing as he was instructed, he was stopped by the guard and was told, "Not you. You stay."

Confused, Derrick asked, "Did I do something wrong?"

"Just shut your fucking mouth and stay here," barked the guard.

The guard stood by the door, and Derrick was all alone in the large, industrial-like laundry facility. The plain, gray concrete floor, the rows of stainless steel laundry machines, and the overwhelming heat was very typical of such a facility in almost any prison. Derrick was only alone for a short time when three other inmates walked in.

As the inmates entered, the guard said to them, "You have exactly thirty minutes before anyone starts asking any questions, so make it fast." They agreed, and the guard left as the three men surrounded Derrick.

"You Derrick Hanson?" asked the inmate who was the obvious ringleader of the trio.

"I am, but listen guys, whatever this might be about, I'm sure we can work something out," said Derrick.

"Not this time."

"Not this time what?" asked Derrick as he was becoming visibly frightened by the confrontation.

"You ain't talking your way out of this shit. Someone on the outside went through a lot of trouble to set this up, and you ain't talking your way out of it."

"Someone went through a lot of trouble to set what up?"

The ringleader smiled, pulled his belt from his pants, and said, "There comes a time when we all need to pay for what we've done in life. It's a time to pay the piper and feel the pain we've caused, and your time is now. It's time, brother," as he folded the belt in half.

Derrick screamed, "Somebody help me!" as he felt the belt slap across his arms as he blocked to protect his face from being struck, but nobody was coming to his rescue.

When a person says the phrase *"for the rest of your life,"* it usually refers to a significant length of time. For Derrick, though, the rest of his life lasted only another twenty-three grueling, painful, horrific minutes, and he met his end with a belt wrapped around his neck.

• • •

Back in their kitchen, Stephanie told Jacob the vague story she had just learned about Derrick's death. Although she didn't have the specific details of what occurred, Jacob's lack of surprise told her he was somehow behind it. She curiously asked, "What do you think happened?"

He pondered before answering, "I'm not sure, but whatever did happen, I'm sure he got what he deserved. In the end, he probably got exactly what he had coming, and he's never going to ruin another life again."

Jacob's response, coupled with the fact that Stephanie had been told Derrick was strangled with a belt, definitely answered her question, and she knew, without the slightest doubt, Jacob was behind whatever occurred in that prison laundry room. In an unexplainable and even somewhat twisted way, Stephanie couldn't have loved Jacob any more than she did at that moment. She knew Jacob was her ultimate protector, and her only reply was, "It's over."

Sometimes, there's just no going back…

The End

ABOUT THE AUTHOR

Anthony Bryan was born and raised in London, U.K., but he spent his adult life in the United States, dividing his time between Boston, Massachusetts and Sarasota, Florida. He served with the United States military in combat operations in Eastern Afghanistan, and it was during his time in war where he developed a true passion for writing.

After returning from Afghanistan, Anthony found himself in a dark place, and he pushed everyone away. It was through his writing where he eventually found internal peace and enjoyment in life once again. Writing became Anthony's Zen.

He has now decided to transform his love of reading and his passion for writing into something for everyone to enjoy. *The Suicide Princess* is just the first of what is certain to become many erotic, romantic, and thrilling works by Anthony – and he hopes you come along with him, every step of the way!

For more information about Anthony, visit:
AnthonyBryanAuthor.com

23297800R00162

Made in the USA
Charleston, SC
19 October 2013